Ruthless!

Book and Lyrics by
Joel Paley

Music by
Marvin Laird

CONCORD
THEATRICALS

FOR PRODUCTION INQUIRIES

UNITED STATES AND CANADA
info@concordtheatricals.com
1-866-979-0447

UNITED KINGDOM AND EUROPE
licensing@concordtheatricals.co.uk
020-7054-7298

Each title is subject to availability from Concord Theatricals Corp., depending upon country of performance. Please be aware that *RUTHLESS!* may not be licensed by Concord Theatricals Corp. in your territory. Professional and amateur producers should contact the nearest Concord Theatricals Corp. office or licensing partner to verify availability.

or gain and whether or not admission is charged. Professional/Stock licensing fees are quoted upon application to Concord Theatricals Corp.

This work is published by Concord Theatricals Corp.

No one shall make any changes in this title(s) for the purpose of production. No part of this book may be reproduced, stored in a retrieval system, scanned, uploaded, or transmitted in any form, by any means, now known or yet to be invented, including mechanical, electronic, digital, photocopying, recording, videotaping, or otherwise, without the prior written permission of the publisher. No one shall share this title(s), or any part of this title(s), through any social media or file hosting websites.

For all inquiries regarding motion picture, television, online/digital and other media rights, please contact Concord Theatricals Corp.

THIRD-PARTY MATERIALS USE NOTE

Licensees are solely responsible for obtaining formal written permission from copyright owners to use copyrighted third-party materials (e.g., incidental music not provided in connection with a performance license, artworks, logos) in the performance of this play and are strongly cautioned to do so. If no such permission is obtained by the licensee, then the licensee must use only original materials and materials that the licensee owns and controls. Licensees are solely responsible and liable for clearances of all third-party copyrighted materials, and shall indemnify the copyright owners of the play(s) and their licensing agent, Concord Theatricals Corp., against any costs, expenses, losses and liabilities arising from the use of such copyrighted third-party materials by licensees. For music, please contact the appropriate music licensing authority in your territory for the rights to any incidental music not provided in connection with a performance license.

IMPORTANT BILLING AND CREDIT REQUIREMENTS

If you have obtained performance rights to this title, please refer to your licensing agreement for important billing and credit requirements.

RUTHLESS! was first produced by Kim Lang Lenny, Wolfgang Bocksch, and Jim Lenny at the Players Theatre in New York, New York, and opened on May 6, 1992. The production was directed and staged by Joel Paley, with musical direction by Marvin Laird, sets by James Noone, costumes by Gail Cooper-Hecht, lights by Kennth Posner, and sound by Tom Source. The stage manager was Pam Edington. The cast was as follows:

SYLVIA ST. CROIX	Joel Vig
JUDY DENMARK	Donna English
TINA DENMARK	Laura Bell Bundy
MISS THORN / MISS BLOCK	Susan Mansur
LOUISE LERMAN / EVE	Joanne Baum
LITA ENCORE	Denise Lor

Understudies:

SYLVIA / MISS THORN / MISS BLOCK / LITA: Lisa McMillan; **JUDY / EVE**: Mary Elizabeth Corcoran; **TINA / LOUISE**: Britney Spears, Natalie Portman

RUTHLESS! was subsequently produced by Joan Stein and Elizabeth Williams at Canon Theatre in Beverly Hills, California, and opened on October 15, 1993. The production was directed and staged by Joel Paley, with musical direction by Nick Vendon, sets by Lawrence Miller, costumes by Bob Mackie, lights by Michael Gilliam, and sound by Michael Cousins. The stage manager was Kathleen Horton. The cast was as follows:

SYLVIA ST. CROIX	Loren Freeman
JUDY DENMARK	Joan Ryan
TINA DENMARK	Lindsay Ridgeway
MISS THORN / MISS BLOCK	Nancy Linari
LOUISE LERMAN / EVE	Joanne Baum
LITA ENCORE	Rita McKenzie

Understudies:

SYLVIA / MISS THORN / MISS BLOCK / LITA: Lisa McMillan; **JUDY**: Joanne Baum; **LOUISE / EVE**: Wendy Coles; **TINA**: Tina Hart

A new streamlined version of *RUTHLESS!* was produced by Maxine Paul, Evan Sacks, and Kenneth Schur at St. Luke's Theatre in New York, New York, and opened on July 13, 2015. The production was directed by Joel Paley, with music direction by Ricky Romano, music supervision and arrangements by Marvin Laird, sets and lighting by Josh Iacovelli, costumes by Nina Vartanian, and sound by John Grosso. The stage manager was Jeremiah Peay. The cast, in order of appearance, was as follows:

SYLVIA ST. CROIX . . . . .Peter Land
JUDY DENMARK . . . . .Kim Maresca
TINA DENMARK . . . . .Tori Murray
MISS THORN . . . . Andrea McCullough
LOUISE LERMAN / EVE . . . . Tracy Jai Edwards
LITA ENCORE. . . . . Rita McKenzie
Understudies:
SYLVIA: Paul Pecorino, Joel Paley; JUDY / MISS THORN / LITA ENCORE: Amie Bermowitz; LOUISE / EVE: Paul Pecorino; TINA: Abigail Harrison

RUTHLESS! was produced in the United Kingdom by Evan Sacks, Darren Bagert, Kenneth Schur, Maxine Paul, and the Menier Chocolate Factory at Arts Theatre, West End, in London, and opened on March 27, 2018. The production was directed by Richard Fitch, with music direction by Simon Beck, choreography by Rebecca Howell, sets and costumes by Morgan Large, lights by Tim Lutkin, and sound by Gregory Clark. The production stage manager was Richard Llewelyn. The cast was as follows:

SYLVIA ST. CROIX . . . . .Jason Gardiner
JUDY DENMARK . . . . .Kim Maresca
TINA DENMARK . . . . Charlotte Breen, Anya Evans,
                                                    Fifi Bloomsbury-Khier, Lucy Simmons
MISS THORN . . . . .Harriet Thrope
LOUISE LERMAN / EVE . . . . Lara Denning
LITA ENCORE. . . . . Tracie Bennett
Understudies:
SYLVIA: Peter Land; JUDY / LOUISE / EVE: Lara Tyrer; MISS THORN / LITA: Lori Haley Fox

Since premiering Off-Broadway some thirty years ago, the show's themes, attitudes and characters have continued to grow more relevant with each passing year. This motivated me to take a deeper dive into the script and lyrics, thus inspiring a number of profoundly exciting and significant revisions. The result was not the creation of a new *Ruthless!* so much as The Stage Mother of All Musicals fully realized!

– J.P.

MUSICAL NUMBERS

ACT I

"Tina's Mother"..Judy

"Born to Entertain"...Tina

"Talent"...Sylvia

"To Play This Part"...Tina

"Teaching Third Grade".................................Miss Thorn

"Where Tina Gets It From".........................Judy & Sylvia

"The Pippi Song"..Louise

"Kisses and Hugs"...................................Tina & Judy

"Teaching Third Grade (Reprise)".......................Miss Thorn

"Talent (Reprise 1)".......................................Sylvia

"I Hate Musicals!"...Lita

"Angel Mom"................................... Sylvia, Judy & Tina

ACT II

"Penthouse Apartment"..Eve

"It Will Never Be That Way Again".........................Ginger

"I Want the Girl"...Sylvia

"There's More to Life".......................................Tina

"Parents and Children"............................Ginger & Tina

"Ruthless!"...Company

"Talent (Reprise 3)".......................................Sylvia

"Talent (Reprise 4)"...Tina

CHARACTERS
(in order of appearance...as they first appear)

SYLVIA ST. CROIX – A stylish woman of a certain age whose histrionic flair secures her a place alongside Mama Rose, Dolly Levi, and Mame as the fourth head carved into the Mount Rushmore of Theatrical Dames. A no-nonsense manager whose specialty is discovering, signing, and guiding the careers of extraordinarily talented children.

JUDY DENMARK – A devoted wife and mother who floats effortlessly through life with a smile, whether doing housework, doting on her daughter, or taking a time-out to bake a cake. Though a woman with opinions on everything from how best to raise her child to preparing a well-balanced meal, she automatically defers to those around her, the result of her hallmark virtue: consummate politeness.

TINA DENMARK – An adorable and talented little girl who knows exactly what she wants to be before she grows up...a big-time Broadway star! When not "on stage" she's sweet, courteous and charmingly manipulates the audience as she manipulates those around her, well aware you draw bees with honey, not vinegar. When she momentarily loses it, she quickly returns to her sweet, innocent persona. Her doing what she does to get what she wants has little to do with being evil and everything to do with her demented sense of entitlement. The longer she plays innocent, the better. Not until Act II, after singing "There's More to Life," does she drop the act completely and bare her sharp ruthless claws.

MISS THORN – Having convinced herself, after years of failing to make it as an actress in New York, that true fulfillment could be found not in front of an audience, but in front of a classroom, she returned to her hometown to become a third-grade teacher. She takes a strict professional approach to putting on the annual school show.

LOUISE LERMAN – An ordinary fourth-grader who likes jumping rope and eating lunch.

LITA ENCORE – A boozy theatre critic who cracks wise, laughs at her own jokes, and can write a review so scathing she can close a Broadway musical in less than two paragraphs. She's a loving and compassionate mother to Judy, whom she adopted and raised as her own child, but can't resist making jokes when engaged in a heart-to-heart talk with her daughter, all in good fun, of course.

EVE – An assistant to a Broadway star, her behavior cycles from professional to erratic to downright bizarre. One minute she's fiercely loyal, the next she's imitating the star's every move, clearly wanting to *be* her, not *work* for her. Her slipping into foreign accents would suggest she marches not to a different drummer, but to an entire drum corp.

FREDERICK DENMARK – Judy's husband, Tina's father, he shows up moments before the final curtain. Although we don't see him, only hear him speak from offstage, it works best having someone deliver his lines live as opposed to using pre-recorded sound cues.

CHARACTER NOTES

Louise Lerman is the only transparent character in the show. All the others are hiding secrets, disguising their true identity, presenting themselves as someone they only think they are, or pretending to be someone they want the world to believe they are. It is essential when playing Sylvia St. Croix or Eve to fully explore their true identity and motivation to disguise themselves. This will impact the actions and reactions of who they're pretending to be.

SETTING

ACT I A safe and friendly suburban neighborhood located in the heart of Any Old Town, USA – the kind of place where people volunteer at hospitals and retirement homes. Socializing means having the neighbors over for a cocktail party, a potluck dinner, or gathering for a spontaneous picnic on a warm Sunday afternoon in Any Old Park. Whole families attend high school football games, and everyone looks forward to seeing their children perform in the annual school show.

ACT II New York City: Neon signs and flashing lights trumpet a glittering metropolis crowded with high-rise buildings, uniformed doormen, and lavish penthouse apartments. Locals and tourists clamor for tickets to Broadway's hot, must-see comedy, poignant drama, or extravagant new musical. And for every performer working on the Great White Way, countless young hopefuls work as waitresses, bellhops, shopgirls, busboys, and bartenders.

TIME

Ruthless! is a fable set in a world before cellphones and the internet, and though it doesn't refer to any one specific era, it evokes a time when people led simpler, more traditional lives. Men were the breadwinners and women took care of the home and the day-to-day raising of the children. Folks listened to the radio for entertainment, theatre tickets were affordable, and the pinnacle of success for a performer was landing a starring role on Broadway.

SETS

ACT I

Prologue

Sylvia's opening remarks are performed in front of the closed main curtain. If there's no main curtain, Sylvia appears in a downstage, off-set pool of light, keeping the Denmark living room as dark as possible.

Denmark Living Room

Essentials

A front door situated for characters to burst through and take center stage. Beyond the door: a garden, a picket fence, etc. Two exits on opposite sides of the stage: one leads to the kitchen, one to the bedrooms. A large picture window, either side of the door; through it we see a bright sunny day and, if possible, characters as they approach the front door.

Furniture

A sofa with coffee table, a club chair with end table (for telephone), a bar with traditional bottles of liquor (one practical). A modest overhead lighting fixture (practical if possible).

Decor

The walls are covered with pictures of Tina, a retro telephone with a receiver connected to the base by a spiral cord, the length of which suits the production, homey knickknacks and touches, e.g. handmade pillows on the sofa, a vase with flowers, a large snow globe, old-fashioned radio, etc.

School Auditorium (No set pieces)

These scenes are played in bright light in front of the closed main curtain. If the venue has no main curtain, the scenes are played far downstage with the Denmark living room as dark as possible.

ACT II

Prologue

Sylvia's courtroom speech and narration are performed in front of the closed main curtain. If there's no main curtain, Sylvia appears in a downstage, off-set pool of light, keeping the penthouse as dark as possible.

Penthouse Apartment

Essentials

An ornate door opens into the penthouse, beyond is a slick hallway that turns at a 45-degree angle, making it possible for Tina to look down the hall and see Frederick, though he's unseen by the audience. A window with a view of the sky, and rooftops of buildings suggest we're high up.

Two exits, on the same side of the stage. One downstage leads to a kitchen, one upstage with a couple of steps up if possible, leading to the bedrooms.

Furniture

A divan, a chrome and leather chair with chrome side table (for telephone), mod-looking bar, hanging chandelier (practical if possible). An ultra-modern look to contrast with the Denmark home.

Decor

The walls are covered with poster-sized photographs of Ginger DelMarco, a faux antique French phone, a prominently displayed Tony Award, modern sculpture, an animal skin area rug, etc.

Alternative to using new furniture for ACT II

The ACT I furniture, minus the coffee table to create a more open space, can be repositioned and redressed to create a modern look. Swap out the homey knickknacks for swank ones. (See Penthouse Decor.)

COSTUMES

General note

The show's seven characters are specific types, with each character given one basic look that defines who they are, except where noted.

ACT I

SYLVIA

Sleek and dramatic. Suggestion: black sparkly top, black skirt showing off her legs, black stockings, black heels. She re-enters Scene Seven wearing a full-length faux fur coat.

JUDY

A fashion magazine housewife, too dressy for housework. Suggestion: bright-patterned dress with a full skirt underdressed with petticoats, light pastel blouse, color-coordinated apron tied around her waist, low heels, single strand of pearls, matching pearl earrings, hair tied back in a tidy bun. While looking feminine, her costume does not reveal her female curves.

TINA

An archetypical child star, whose hair ribbons match the ruffle on her socks and the bows on her tap shoes. Lots of crinoline poofing out her dress. Suggestion: red with white polka dots, pink trim. She enters wearing tap shoes, changes into Mary Janes (preset) after "Born to Entertain." For *Pippi* rehearsal, same dress with unflattering long, droopy brown dog ears attached to a beret.

MISS THORN

The appearance of someone who long ago gave up on how she looks. Suggestion: muted skirt, plain blouse, sweater worn over her shoulders, hair in a top bun with a pencil sticking out. For her entrance in Scene Seven, she wears over-sized dark glasses.

LOUISE LERMAN

Scene Two: Like her personality: drab. Suggestion: Green culottes, brown sweater, clunky shoes. Scene Six: dress rehearsal: a shipwrecked Pippi Longstocking. Suggestion: Bright-red Pippi wig with pigtails that stick out, red and white-striped stockings, one up, one rolled down, overalls draped with seaweed and assorted ocean detritus.

LITA ENCORE

Professional chic. Suggestion: a handsome tailored skirt-suit and a jaunty hat.

ACT II

SYLVIA

Prologue: Suggestion: same skirt, black and white sequined blouse. When entering the penthouse she wears her fur coat, and black and white turban-style hat. (See Specifics.)

GINGER DELMARCO

Judy's transformation to Ginger, the most significant character change in the show, is a startling head-to-toe makeover from a demure housewife to a strutting, glamorous Broadway star. Suggestion: first appears in a full-length silk kimono and a pair of fuzzy mules (for the Prologue). She returns wearing high heels and, under the kimono, a sultry, beaded knockout-of-a-dress, short and tantalizingly low-cut. Her hair, an overly-large, exaggerated flip.

EVE

Professional, put together. Suggestion: simple skirt, crisp white, ruffled blouse, half heels, hair pulled back in a neat bun. When she comes on for the "Ruthless!" number, she wears the dress Ginger tossed at her: a red, low-cut number, very short with a slit up the side, high heels, her hair down in an obvious attempt to resemble Ginger.

TINA

She hasn't changed. Suggestion: the exact same Act I outfit, only now made out of black and white-striped material suggesting a traditional prison uniform.

LITA

She'd rather drink than shop. Suggestion: the same outfit as ACT I.

MISS THORN

Her idea of how a serious artist of the theatre dresses. Suggestion: black stretch pants, an off-the-shoulder angora sweater, a French beret, dance shoes.

The Props

The script mentions the basic props needed, leaving it to the director and choreographer's imagination to add things e.g. a mop for Judy ("Tina's Mother") and a feather duster for Eve to pretend to use ("Penthouse Apartment"), etc.

Some Specifics

Sylvia's lightning-fast reveal as Ruth DelMarco

It's difficult to wear a secured wig on top of another secured wig and have the top wig removed quickly. The brilliant Bob Mackie solved this problem when he designed the costumes for the premiere Los Angeles production. During intermission, Sylvia's shoulder-length platinum gray wig is secured in place. For the Act II Prologue, she wears her original wig over the gray wig, with enough pins to hold it in place during the short scene. During "Penthouse Apartment," Sylvia replaces the Act I wig with a snug-fitting turban that has bits and pieces of hair that match the ACT I wig sewn into the brim, enough hair peeking out to create the illusion that she has the same hair under the turban. For the reveal, she whips off the turban and reveals the gray wig securely in place, enabling her to whip her head around, dramatically exposing her gray, shoulder-length bob.

The gun
The gun Eve pulls on Ginger should be identical to the water pistol Louise uses as Pippi Longstocking for three reasons: 1) It's funnier when an obvious toy gun is responsible for the shoot-'em-up denouement. 2) Using a small plastic gun makes it easier for Eve to secure it on her person and get to it quickly. 3) Eve turns out to be Betty Lerman, therefore having the same actor playing the doomed kid and her doomed mother, whipping out the same gun creates an undeniable sense of absurd theatrical poetry.

AUTHORS' NOTES

A Note About Casting

The show has seven female characters and works best performed with six actors, one doubling as Louise Lerman in ACT I, and Eve, who ultimately reveals herself as Louise's mother, in ACT II.

For the original Off-Broadway production, we wanted an all-female cast, and though we had no trouble finding actors for most of the roles, after extensive auditioning we hadn't found a female who embodied all of Sylvia St. Croix's characteristics: a commanding presence, her articulate sense of theatricality, alternately confident and desperate, and an ever-present air of mystery. While working on a Theatre Guild *Theatre at Sea* cruise, we saw Joel Vig perform a parody of a provocative female nightclub singer. We found our Sylvia. The talented Mr. Vig was cast solely for his ability to play the character with passion and integrity. Aside from some chuckling at a guy in high heels, we were convinced audiences would see him as the formidable Sylvia St. Croix regardless of his "plumbing."

This leap of faith made it clear; all the characters in *Ruthless!* are just that...*characters*. None of the roles call for gender- or age-specific casting. The show will work with all females, all males, or any combination of both. (Adults, male and female, have played eight-year-old Tina Denmark.) The one unequivocal casting rule is to find actors who will play their character genuinely instead of going for obvious easy laughs. Outrageous and irrational characters taking themselves and the situations they're in seriously is key to performing a demented theatrical fable.

Talent That Dares Not Speak Its Name

When Sylvia mentions *talent* as being passed down from generation to generation, she's not speaking about inheriting creative skills, but rather a talent corrupted by a pathological need to be famous. So enamored by the tidal waves of love crashing over the footlights, these gifted souls become adulation junkies, addicted to standing ovations and consumed by an endless need to be loved and adored by everyone, everywhere, all the time. And nothing is more harrowing than when this mania affects a little girl, spawning a child so fierce she'll do anything...*anything* to be the apple of everyone's eye. Such is the ruthless exploitation of something as lovely and as precious as talent.

If You Laugh, The Audience Won't!

The characters in the show are never aware they're performing in a comedy. They don't hold for laughs because nothing they do or say (or sing) is funny to them, only to the audience. The situations they find themselves in are dramatic and grow more intense as the story unfolds.

Rhythm and Pacing

The show is performed as a farce. Fast and furious, it charges on, except for the designated *beats* and *pauses*. That's not to say every moment and emotion isn't given its full dramatic value, it's simply that the world the characters inhabit moves at a faster RPM than real life. The tone is that of the screwball comedies of the thirties and forties where everyone instantly knows what to say and says it. The story moves at a clip, staying well ahead of audiences rather than letting their reaction dictate the pacing. Creating the illusion that Act II moves at the same pace as Act I requires playing it at a slightly quicker pace, which continues to accelerate until the final curtain. Even the dramatic "ballads" in Act II are sung posthaste.

Breaking the Forth Wall

There are times when the script calls for a character to break the fourth wall. These moments are selected judiciously. They're not meant as an invitation for characters to acknowledge the audience whenever the mood strikes them. Doing so would lessen the surprising effect of breaking the fourth wall when indicated in the script.

Effective Sound Effects

Throughout the show, the sounds of ringing telephones and doorbells are integral to a song or used to create a feeling of anticipation when interrupting an onstage moment. Both, therefore, must resonate with presence and volume! There should be a characteristic distinction between the ACT I and ACT II telephone rings and doorbell chimes.

A Note to Actors

Bernadette Peters gave a magnificent performance as Judy Denmark when *Ruthless!* was presented as a staged reading to benefit Equity Fights Aids. (Check out the clips available on YouTube.) Her understanding of the material is as good as it gets, so I've invited her to address the actors directly. "Bernadette...?"

"Thank you, Joel.

"*Ruthless!* is a show that could be labeled as *camp*. The important thing to remember when playing camp, or any comedy, is it must be played real. When the words themselves are funny, you don't have to do anything but deliver them in character, the words themselves will take care of the humor.

"Early on in my career I played Ruby in *Dames at Sea*, a pastiche of old Hollywood movie musicals, a production that was also labelled as camp. Our wonderful director, Neal Kenyan, gave the cast an important note, one that has stayed with me throughout my career. '*Dames at Sea* is your friend...and you don't make fun of your friends.' If you work to make every moment, no matter how silly or outrageous, as real as can be, I promise you will have a fun and successful experience."

– B.P.

"Thanks Bernadette. I love those shoes!" If anyone has questions, comments, or would like to send photos of your production, email me at frederickdenmark11@gmail.com.

– J.P.

Over the years many people have contributed their time and considerable talents to every aspect of *Ruthless!* To thank them all individually would require more pages than the script itself. Just know we love you and thank you (You know who you are!) from the bottom of our hearts.

We are tremendously grateful to those who played a unique role in breathing life into *Ruthless!*: Joanne Baum, Tracie Bennett, Lorna Bundy, Lynn Cohen, Dame Gillian Lynn, Maxine Paul, Bernadette Peters, Ricky Romano, Stephen Sondheim, Joan Stein, Tony Stimac, and Douglas Wood.

We greatly appreciate Abbie Van Nostrand, Amy Rose Marsh, David Geer, Zachary Orts, Nicole Matte, Fiona Kyle, and everyone at Concord Theatricals. Not only because they love and respect what a script is, but for their enthusiastically sharing our vision of what a script can become!

Our deepest and heartfelt thanks to Ken Sacks who, by encouraging and supporting him every step of the way, made it possible for his twin brother, Evan, to be on this *Ruthless!* journey.

Kisses and Hugs,
Joel and Marvin

ACT I

(Prologue: **SYLVIA ST. CROIX** *appears in front of the curtain, addresses the audience.)*

SYLVIA. Talent! Where does it come from? Good evening. My name is Sylvia St. Croix.

[MUSIC NO. 00 "UNDERSCORE"]

Where *does* talent come from? Is it a product of one's environment? Something you pick up in the street? Or is talent something you're born with. Something passed down from generation to generation. Something in the blood. *(Beat.)* Meet Judy Denmark.

[MUSIC NO. 00A "UNDERSCORE"]

*(***JUDY DENMARK*** *enters from the kitchen, carrying a breakfast tray. She poses, smiles.)*

Pretty, isn't she?

*(***JUDY*** *sits on the sofa, sets the tray on the coffee table, and pours a cup of coffee.)*

A wife and mother living an idyllic suburban life. And, although Judy has no talent whatsoever, her only child, her daughter, Tina, has been blessed with a great deal of talent. Who could've guessed that one day little Tina would... *(Phone rings.)* But I'm getting ahead of myself. *(Exits.)*

[MUSIC NO. 01 "TINA'S MOTHER"]

1

Scene One

(The Denmark living room. Morning.)

JUDY.

    I'LL GET IT.

(Phone rings again, she answers.)

HELLO

YES, THIS IS TINA'S MOTHER

HELLO, MRS. MILLER

HOW'S THAT?

TINA BROUGHT YOU FLOWERS FROM OUR GARDEN

WELL, SHE'S SO FOND OF YOU

SHE LIKES YOUR HUSBAND TOO!

THANK YOU FOR CALLING

GOOD-BYE

(Hangs up, starts for sofa, phone rings.)

I'll get it. *(Answers phone.)*

HELLO

YES, THIS IS TINA'S MOTHER

HELLO, MRS. FARMER

HOW'S THAT?

TINA SANG AND DANCED FOR YOUR BLIND MOTHER?

SHE LOVES TO ENTERTAIN

YOU SAY SHE TOOK HER CANE?

THANK YOU FOR CALLING

GOOD-BYE

(Hangs up, phone rings, she answers.)

TINA'S MOTHER HERE
HI, MRS. ADAMS
A PARTY?
I'LL TELL HER SHE'S INVITED

(Hangs up, phone rings, she answers.)

TINA'S MOTHER HERE
SORRY, MRS. ADAMS
SATURDAY AT FOUR
I'M SURE SHE'LL BE DELIGHTED
BYE *(Hangs up.)*
I COULD'VE BEEN AN OFFICE GIRL
A WIZARD AT DICTATION
WORKING FIFTY WEEKS A YEAR
TWO WEEKS PAID VACATION
I COULD'VE BEEN A TEACHER
TEACHING ONE THING OR ANOTHER
BUT I'M PROUD TO BE WHAT I AM...
TINA'S MOTHER!

(Phone rings, she answers.)

HELLO
YES, THIS IS TINA'S MOTHER
HELLO, PASTOR PETERS
HOW'S THAT?
TINA HAS A CHOIR SOLO SUNDAY
OH HOW SHE LOVES TO SING
OF COURSE SHE LOVES TO PRAY
SHE'S GOOD AT EVERYTHING
I'M GRATEFUL EVERY DAY
WHY, EVERYONE AGREES
SHE'S POSITIVELY HEAVEN-SENT
MY KID'S THE PERFECT EIGHT-YEAR-OLD
YES, SHE'S ENTHRALLING
THANK YOU FOR CALLING
GOOD-BYE

(Hangs up, doorbell chimes.)

I'll get it.

(JUDY floats to the door, opens it. SYLVIA is wearing dark glasses.)

SYLVIA. Mrs. Denmark? Mrs. Judy Denmark?

JUDY. Why, yes. I'm Judy. I'm Judy Denmark. Judy Denmark, that's my name! Judy! Judy Denmark!

SYLVIA. Tina's mother?

JUDY.
THAT'S ME!

SYLVIA. My card. *(Hands JUDY her business card, sweeps into room.)*

JUDY. I'm afraid mine are being printed. *(Closes door.)*

SYLVIA. My, what a lovely home.

JUDY. Thank you... *(Reading business card.)* ...Miss St. Croix.

SYLVIA. Please, call me Sylvia.

JUDY. Sylvia St. Croix. Are you French?

SYLVIA. St. Croix is my stage name. I was born Lady Sylvia St. Francis of Assisi. What beautiful curtains.

JUDY. Thank you, Sylvia.

SYLVIA. That's a pretty dress.

JUDY. Thank you, Sylvia.

SYLVIA. *(Eyeing the breakfast tray.)* And doesn't this look delicious.

JUDY. It's just toast, Sylvia.

SYLVIA. Denmark. What sort of name is Denmark?

JUDY. Danish?

SYLVIA. No, thanks. The toast is fine. *(Snags a piece of toast.)* Is your husband at home? *(Nibbles.)*

JUDY. *(Calls offstage.)* Frederick? *(Beat.)* I'm afraid not.

SYLVIA. Working?

JUDY. I hope so.

SYLVIA. Pity. I do like speaking with both parents. When will he be returning?

JUDY. I'm not sure.

SYLVIA. What does Mr. Denmark do?

JUDY. I don't know.

SYLVIA. Well, whatever it is, you're a lucky girl, Judy Denmark.

JUDY. I know. I'm a Libra!

SYLVIA. This lovely home, a successful husband and, of course, the very reason I'm here, your daughter...Tina.

[MUSIC NO. 01A "UNDERSCORE"]

I caught her performance last Saturday at the Rolling Hills Twilight Home for the Elderly. Sensational!

JUDY. We're very proud of our daughter.

SYLVIA. It was a triumph!

JUDY. If you like, I can arrange for her to perform for all of you again next Saturday.

SYLVIA. I don't live there, Mrs. Denmark. I was visiting an elderly friend.

JUDY. Would you like to meet her?

SYLVIA. I'd love to.

JUDY. She's outside breaking in her new tap shoes.

[MUSIC NO. 02 "BORN TO ENTERTAIN"]

(**JUDY** *calls out window.*)

Tina, you're on!

(**JUDY** *opens the front door.* **TINA DENMARK** *bursts in, runs downstage center.* **JUDY** *closes the door.*)

TINA. Hello, Mother!

JUDY. Darling, we have company.

TINA. (*Taking in the audience.*) I love company!

JUDY. Say hello to Miss St. Croix.

(**TINA** *performs a short tap break, waves to* **SYLVIA.**)

TINA. Hi!

JUDY. Tina loves to perform.

TINA.
SOME GIRLS LIKE TO COOK AND SEW
WHEN I COOK IT'S IN A SHOW
I WAS BORN TO ENTERTAIN!

(*To audience member.*) How ya doin'? (*Cuts them off.*) It's a rhetorical question!
SOME GIRLS PREFER TO HELP MOM CLEAN
I'D RATHER LEARN A DANCE ROUTINE
I WAS BORN TO ENTERTAIN!

(*To audience member.*) Where ya from? (*Motions for music to stop.*) No, really, where ya from? (*Cuts them off.*) I'm kidding!
INSTEAD OF WALKIN' I GO FLAPPIN'
WHEN I TAP I MAKE IT HAPPEN

MOM SAYS I GOT BROADWAY ON THE BRAIN
DON'T GET TOO COMFY IN THAT SEAT
WHEN I STRUT MY STUFF
YOU'LL BE ON YOUR FEET
I WAS BORN TO SING AND DANCE!
BREAK!

(Performs a tap routine.)

NOT EVERY SHOW-BIZ CINDERELLA
HAS GOT TO COME FROM POCATELLO
MY STAR WILL RISE LIKE BUBBLES IN CHAMPAGNE
BY NOW YOU GUESSED MY ONE AMBITION
IS NOT TO BE NO MATHEMATICIAN
I WAS BORN TO AMUSE
FROM THE TIP OF MY NOSE
TO THE TAP OF MY SHOES
STRIKE UP THE BAND
HAND ME A HAT AND MY CANE

The one I took from the blind lady!
I WAS BORN TO ENTERTAIN!

SYLVIA. That was wonderful, dear. Brava!

TINA. *(Curtsies.)* Thank you, Madam St. Croix.

SYLVIA. Please, call me Sylvia.

TINA. All right, Sylvia. Judy?

JUDY. Very good, Tina. And, please, call me Mommy.

SYLVIA. Tina, how would you like to be a star?

[MUSIC NO. 02A "UNDERSCORE"]

TINA. It's all I've ever wanted. More than anything in the world!

SYLVIA. Well, that's why I'm here. I work with gifted-specially children. I plan careers as well as develop talent. You are planning a professional career for your daughter, are you not?

JUDY. We want her to finish school first.

SYLVIA. Of course. What time does she get out? Three?

JUDY. I wasn't just talking about today.

SYLVIA. *(Disappointed.)* Oh.

JUDY. We want our daughter to have a normal childhood.

TINA. Maybe it's time to move on?

SYLVIA. What do you say?

TINA. Please, Mama. I want to be good.

JUDY. You are good, baby.

TINA. I want to be gooder!

JUDY. I really think she should stay in school. Let me discuss it with my husband.

TINA. Oh, poop! Daddy's never home.

JUDY. Tina, you just saw Daddy six weeks ago.

TINA. That was Daddy?

JUDY. I think so.

SYLVIA. Your daughter's good, Mrs. Denmark. With my help, she will be great.

JUDY. I think having a good education will give her something to fall back on.

SYLVIA. And that's precisely what she'll do the moment the going gets tough. I believe when you have nothing to fall back on, you simply don't fall back.

JUDY. But childhood is a time for playing with dolls and riding a bike.

[MUSIC NO. 03 "TALENT"]

SYLVIA.

OH, ANY TYKE CAN RIDE A BIKE
ANY BRAT CAN SWING A BAT
EVERY MOTHER'S CHILD PLAYS WITH BLOCKS
THEY RUN AND SKIP AND JUMP
AND CLIMB ON ROCKS
THAT MAY BE TRUE FOR EVERY DICK AND JANE
AH, BUT SOME OF US WERE BORN TO ENTERTAIN!

(To herself.) This time I'm doing it for you, baby!

(To **TINA.***)* YOU CAN HAVE IT ALL
YOU'VE GOT TALENT
LIFE CAN BE A BALL
IF YOU'VE GOT TALENT

WHEN IT'S OBVIOUS YOUR CHILD'S NOT
AN AVERAGE ORDINARY TOT
SHOWER HER WITH LOVE AND VALIDATION
JUDY, RECOGNIZE HER SPECIALTIES
HER OPPORTUNITY TO SEIZE
THE BRASS RING OF SUCCESS
ACCLAIM AND ADORATION

(To **TINA.***)* Come 'ere. Do you like ice cream?

TINA. You bet I do!

SYLVIA.

IT'S ALL BANANA SPLITS
WHEN YOU'VE GOT TALENT
YOU DON'T HAVE TO SHOW YOUR TITS
IF YOU GOT TALENT!
YOU'RE NO SILLY PLASTIC INGÉNUE
IN CHEESY ADS FOR CHEAP SHAMPOO
DARLING, YOU'RE TOO GOOD FOR TELEVISION
I'M TALKING STRAIGHT LEGIT
I MEAN THE BROADWAY STAGE

THE SILVER SCREEN
BUT FIRST WE NEED YOUR MOTHER
TO MAKE THE RIGHT DECISION...

TINA. Oh, Mother, please!

SYLVIA. *(Covers* **TINA***'s ears.)* She's not getting any younger.

JUDY. I suppose some coaching can't hurt. But only after school.

SYLVIA. We start this afternoon!

JUDY. I'm afraid she can't this afternoon.

TINA. Today I'm auditioning for the school show. I'm trying out for the lead.

JUDY. Do you have children, Sylvia?

[MUSIC NO. 03A "UNDERSCORE / TALENT"]

SYLVIA. I prefer not to discuss it, Mrs. Denmark.

JUDY. I'm sorry...

SYLVIA. Let's just say the child had no talent.

JUDY. I didn't mean –

SYLVIA. Not what I call talent! Oh, when we had company, she'd start jumping around the living room yelling, "Look, everyone! I'm dancing! I'm dancing!" She wasn't dancing. She was jumping! It was humiliating.
(To **TINA***.)* IT CANNOT BE DENIED
YOU'VE GOT TALENT
AND I'LL BE BY YOUR SIDE
TO GUIDE THAT TALENT
SO, KICK UP YOUR HEELS AND TAP YOUR TOES
I'M YOUR AUNTIE MAME! YOUR MAMA ROSE!
AND NOTHING'S GONNA STOP US TILL WE'RE THROUGH
HONEY, SYLVIA WILL MAKE YOUR DREAM COME TRUE
YOU'VE GOT TALENT

SO MUCH TALENT
BABY, YOU'LL HAVE IT ALL
WAIT AND SEE
FOR ALONG WITH ALL THAT TALENT
YOU'VE GOT...

(Catches **JUDY***'s eye.)* Your mother...

JUDY. Thank you.

SYLVIA.

AND ME!

(Blackout.)

[MUSIC NO. 03B "SCENE CHANGE"]

Scene Two

(Turner school auditorium. Later that afternoon.)

(School bell rings, lights up on **MISS THORN**. *She addresses the audience as students.)*

MISS THORN. Good afternoon, children. I'm Miss Thorn, the director of last year's gripping production of *Who's Afraid of Virginia Woolf, Jr.* This year the school is delighted to be presenting the world premiere of a new musical, *Pippi in Tahiti*, written and directed by me, Myrna Thorn. Thank you.

Oh, and do let me know whose mother can bring a box of cookies and a case of red wine to what promises to be a thrilling evening of musical theatre. Let's begin.

*(***TINA*** enters, crosses center.)*

Please welcome third-grader, Tina Denmark. *(Steps to one side.)*

[MUSIC NO. 04 "TO PLAY THIS PART"]

TINA.
TO DANCE MY DANCES
TO SING MY SONG
IT'S ALL I'VE WANTED
ALL I'VE DREAMED
MY WHOLE LIFE LONG
NOW THAT DREAM IS COMING TRUE
IT'S TIME FOR MY DEBUT
DO I WANT THIS? YES I DO!
WITH ALL MY HEART
IT MEANS EVERYTHING
TO PLAY THIS PART

MISS THORN. Thank you, Tina.

> (**TINA** *exits,* **MISS THORN** *motions into the*
> *wings.*)

Hang on, Rachel. I am pleased to announce our cast
has been invited on a school trip to New York City to
see a matinee performance of *Henry VI, Part Two*,
followed by dinner at the world-famous Olive Garden,
Times Square! Now here's Rachel Hobbs.

> (**MISS THORN** *exits,* **TINA** *steps out from the*
> *wings.*)

TINA.
> I LOVE PUPPIES
> AND SANTA CLAUS
> BUT THEY DON'T HOLD A CANDLE
> TO APPLAUSE
> I PRAY TO YOU ON HIGH
> THE CASTING AGENT IN THE SKY
> CAST ME! C'MON!
> I'LL STAY TRUE TO MY ART
> PLAYING PIPPI, DARE I SAY
> IS MY TICKET TO BROADWAY
> IT MEANS EVERYTHING
> TO PLAY THIS PART

> (**TINA** *remains onstage.* **MISS THORN** *enters.*)

MISS THORN. I want to thank all our talented students,
and some of our not-so-talented ones. Really, Rachel
Hobbs, what on earth were you doing? This year we
are fortunate indeed. Not only is Mike Lerman, owner
of Lerman's Hardware, donating all the materials, he's
going to build our sets. And his wife, Betty Lerman,
along with all the gals at Betty's Needle Nook, is
designing and making our costumes!

[MUSIC NO. 04A "UNDERSCORE"]

And now, boys and girls, the starring role of Pippi Longstocking will be played by... (**TINA** *starts for center stage.*) ...Miss Louise Lerman!

> (**TINA** *freezes as* **LOUISE LERMAN** *enters and bows.*)

TINA. *(Beat.)* Are you fucking kidding me?[*]

> *(School bell rings. Blackout.)*

[MUSIC NO. 04B "SCENE CHANGE"]

---

[*]If for some reason you can't drop the F-bomb, **TINA** should mouth the word, which can be censored with a beep tone. Do not pick a different word.

Scene Three

(Denmark living room. One hour later.)

*(**TINA** is collapsed on the sofa, mouth open, staring at the ceiling.)*

SYLVIA. You had your heart set on playing Pippi.

TINA. It's the title role.

JUDY. Tina...

TINA. It's the best part in the show.

SYLVIA. The only part if you ask me.

JUDY. Sweetheart...

TINA. I don't understand. *(Makes an innocent casting remark.)* Louise Lerman is too Jewish-looking to play Pippi.

SYLVIA. She has no fire! No music!

JUDY. So what if you're not playing Pippi. You get to play Puddles.

TINA. I don't want to play her dog!

SYLVIA. Puddles doesn't sing! Puddles doesn't talk! Puddles is a stupid mime part.

TINA. I hate mime.

SYLVIA. Who doesn't?

TINA. I know why Louise Lerman got the part. And it's not fair. *(Getting angry.)* I was born to play Pippi Longstocking!

JUDY. Listen, young lady. This is not the end of the world.

TINA. *(Suddenly sweet.)* You're right, Mother. I only wanted that silly old part so you and Daddy would be proud of me.

JUDY. We are proud of you, Tina. Of course, if you had gotten the part, we would've been real, *real* proud, but nevertheless...

TINA. Oh, Mother, what would you give me for a shower of kisses?

JUDY. I'd give you a tub of hugs.

(Doorbell chimes.)

TINA. I'll get it.

[MUSIC NO. 04C "UNDERSCORE"]

*(**TINA** runs and opens the door.)*

MISS THORN. Good afternoon, Tina.

TINA. *(Curtsying.)* Good afternoon, Miss Thorn.

MISS THORN. That was an excellent curtsy.

TINA. *(Curtsying.)* Thank you, Miss Thorn.

MISS THORN. *(To **JUDY**.)* She's so polite.

JUDY. *(Curtsying.)* Thank you, Miss Thorn.

MISS THORN. And I see where she gets it from.

JUDY & TINA. *(Curtsying.)* Thank you, Miss Thorn.

TINA. I knew you'd change your mind. Mommy! Mommy! I'm playing Pippi!

MISS THORN. I'm afraid not, dear.

TINA. Afraid? Afraid of what? Let's go, Sylvia. *(Exits.)*

*(**SYLVIA** starts for the door.)*

JUDY. Won't you sit down, Miss Thorn?

MISS THORN. *(Curtsying.)* No, thank you, Mrs. Denmark.

SYLVIA. *(Pauses at door.)* Excuse me, who do we speak to about comps?

MISS THORN. Sorry. No free tickets. School policy.

SYLVIA. I bet the Lerman kid gets comps! *(Exits.)*

JUDY. Thank you for coming. The reason I've asked you here –

MISS THORN. I know what's on your mind, Mrs. Denmark, and no, I'm not a lesbian. *(Beat.)* Okay, I may have experimented in college. Didn't we all?

JUDY. You were an actress before you began teaching?

MISS THORN. I was.

JUDY. Was there ever a part you wanted but didn't get?

MISS THORN. What's your point?

JUDY. Tina's awfully upset about not playing Pippi.

[MUSIC NO. 05 "TEACHING THIRD GRADE"]

MISS THORN. I must admit, in all my years as a professional actress, and I've worked on both coasts, I've never known anyone to want a part so desperately. It's as if starring in the school show means too much to Tina.

JUDY. That's what worries me.

MISS THORN.
THERE'S NO NEED TO WORRY
UNKNIT YOUR BROW
FOR THOUGH TINA'S
TAKING IT HARD RIGHT NOW
EXPERIENCE TELLS ME I'M HAPPY TO SAY
SHE'LL GET OVER HER DISAPPOINTMENT...
SOMEDAY

She'll learn starring in the school show, or on Broadway, isn't the only game in town. Life is full of wonderful opportunities just as exciting and far more rewarding. Look at me...

TEACHING THIRD GRADE
SHAPING THE MINDS

OF A NEW GENERATION
RELAXED, UNAFRAID
EVERY DAY A DELIGHT...
WITH THE RIGHT MEDICATION

SURE, I RAN TO NEW YORK
A FIRE BURNING IN MY BELLY
I HAD IT ALL JUST LIKE THAT
WHAT'S-HER-FACE...MINNELLI
I GAVE 'EM MY BEST
THEY WEREN'T IMPRESSED
THE ONLY ROLES I GOT
WERE ONION ROLLS AT THE DELI
YOU'VE MADE IT CLEAR, LORD
MY PLACE IS HERE, LORD
TEACHING THIRD GRADE

JUDY. So you agree someone in show business should have something to fall back on?

MISS THORN. Oh, yes! Yes indeed!
SOMETHING TO FALL BACK ON
LESSON NUMBER ONE
THAT'S HOW I BECAME
WHO I'VE BECOME
AT NIGHT I GET COZY
POUR WINE, LIGHT THE TAPERS
TWO BOTTLES OF MERLOT
I'M NAKED IN BED GRADING PAPERS
THE PAYCHECK IS STEADY
MY SUMMERS ARE FREE
WHO NEEDS THE LIMELIGHT
WHEN YOU CAN BE ME?

HAVING FALLEN BACK ON SOMETHING
SURE, I'M SAFE AND I'M SECURE
THAT'S ALL I AM! THAT'S IT!
THERE AIN'T NOTHING MORE
NOT ONLY AM I LONELY

    I DESPERATELY NEED TO GET LAID
    GOD IT'S SO GODDAMN TEDIOUS
    TEACHING THIRD GRADE!

JUDY. Would you look at the time.

MISS THORN.
    I'M SICK OF SALLY, SICK OF DICKY
    NEVER QUIET, ALWAYS STICKY

JUDY. I wonder what's keeping them?

MISS THORN.
    NOSES RUNNY, NOSES BLEEDY
    LITTLE RUNTS SO BLOODY NEEDY

JUDY. Can I get you a drink? A Xanax, maybe?

MISS THORN.
    WHAT, ARE YOU KIDDING?
    I'D LOVE ONE INDEED!
    BUT BOOZE AND NARCOTICS
    ARE NOT WHAT I NEED, I NEED...
    SOMETHING TO FALL BACK ON
    FROM WHAT I'VE FALLEN BACK ON!

JUDY. About Tina...?

MISS THORN. Mrs. Denmark...
    NO ONE LOOKS FORWARD TO FEELING UPSET
    BUT SOONER OR LATER EVERYONE GETS WET
    TODAY IT'S RAINING ON TINA'S PARADE
    LIFE IS A BITCH...
    AND IT STARTS IN THIRD GRADE!

        (*SYLVIA enters with* **TINA***, who's sipping a
        super-sized soda through a long straw.*)

SYLVIA. Miss Thorn, why not let Tina be Pippi Longstocking's
understudy?

TINA. What's an understudy?

SYLVIA. An understudy is an actor who learns the part and plays it if the star can't go on.

MISS THORN. We're only giving the one performance, but why not. Tina, you can be Pippi's understudy.

JUDY. Isn't that nice?

TINA. You mean I would learn all of Pippi's songs and dances, and all of Pippi's lines, and I might not get to play Pippi in the show?

MISS THORN. That's correct.

SYLVIA. Unless, of course, something were to happen to Louise Lerman.

[MUSIC NO. 05A "UNDERSCORE"]

(TINA *sips her soda thoughtfully. Sound: straw sipping.)*

TINA. *(Smiles.)* I'll do it.

(Lights fade.)

[MUSIC NO. 05B "SCENE CHANGE"]

Scene Four

(Turner auditorium stage. Three weeks later.)

*(**MISS THORN** is having little success teaching **LOUISE** simple choreography. **TINA** sits to one side, watching.)*

MISS THORN.
   AGAIN!

LOUISE. Can you make the dance easier?

MISS THORN. Anything easier would be walking. Now follow along. *(Demonstrating steps)* Step left...

LOUISE. *(In agreement.)* Right.

MISS THORN. Cross right, then step left...

LOUISE. Right.

MISS THORN. Step right, kick left...

LOUISE. Right.

   Kick left, right? Or kick right? No, left. Right? What?

MISS THORN. Are you on something?

LOUISE. Not anymore.

MISS THORN. Can you get back on it? Tina? Demonstrate?

TINA. *(Stands.)* I'm not warmed up, but let's give it a go. Five! Six! Seven! Eight!

[MUSIC NO. 05C "DANCE COMBINATION"]

*(**TINA** nails the combination.)*

MISS THORN. Sheer perfection.

LOUISE. Are we done? Can I go home?

MISS THORN. Again! Step left, cross right...

LOUISE. My stomach hurts.

(Lights fade out.)

[MUSIC NO. 05D "SCENE CHANGE"]

Scene Five

(Denmark living room. Afternoon, three weeks later.)

SYLVIA. That was a delicious lunch, dear. Thank you for inviting me.

JUDY. Well, you've been here since breakfast.

SYLVIA. Judy, I envy you. I wish I had a little girl.

JUDY. I thought you said –

SYLVIA. *(Sharply.)* A talented one!

JUDY. Would you like to talk about it?

[MUSIC NO. 06 "WHERE TINA GETS IT FROM"]

SYLVIA. What is there to say? You would think one's own flesh and blood would have inherited at least a fraction of her mother's talent.

JUDY. Who's to say where talent comes from? Look at Tina. After all…

I CAN'T SING A NOTE
NO TALENT WHATSOEVER
I CAN'T TELL A JOKE
I'M SIMPLY NOT THAT CLEVER
MAKE NO MISTAKE
WITH PRIDE I'M OVERCOME
BUT I HAVEN'T A CLUE
AS TO WHO
TINA GETS IT FROM

SYLVIA. Surely there's something you can do.

JUDY. Let me think…
I CAN MAKE A BED
AND FRICASSEE A CHICKEN

SYLVIA. You're brimming with talent.

JUDY.

MY SWEET ONION SPREAD
WHEN SPREAD ON GARLIC BREAD
IS FINGER LICKIN'
BUT ON A STAGE
I SIMPLY WOULD GO NUMB
SO I'M UP IN THE AIR
AS TO WHERE
TINA GETS IT FROM

SYLVIA.

LEAVE EVERYTHING TO ME, DEAR
I'VE BEEN AROUND THE BLOCK
AS LONG AS SHE MAKES MILLIONS
WHO CARES WHERE TINA GETS IT FROM
NOW, HERE'S THE WAY WE PLAY IT
FIRST WE SIGN WITH AGENTS
ONE IN NEW YORK
ONE ON THE COAST

JUDY.

SYLVIA	JUDY
SHE'S GREAT FOR A TALK SHOW	HEY! STOP BY FOR SOME CHICKEN
BUT ONLY A COUPLE OVEREXPOSURE IS	
ALL TOO COMMON IN THE HIGHLY COMPETITIVE WORLD	MY... SWEET ONION SPREAD
WHERE A PROFESSIONAL KID	WHEN SPREAD
WILL MAKE MORE MONEY THAN HER PARENTS	ON GARLIC BREAD IS FINGER LICKIN'
A STAR AS BRIGHT AS SHE, DEAR...	BUT ON A STAGE
ONE BRIGHTER THAN THE SUN	I SIMPLY WOULD GO NUMB
HER FANS EVERYWHERE	SO I'M UP IN THE AIR

SYLVIA.	JUDY.
SIMPLY WON'T CARE WHERE	AS TO WHERE MY
TINA GETS IT FROM	TINA GETS IT FROM
	NO MATTER WHERE SHE GOT IT

OH, WHO CARES?
YOUR KID IS GONNA EARN A LOT

SYLVIA & JUDY.
IT DOESN'T MATTER, NO!
IT MATTERS NOT
NOT A BIT, NOT A CRUMB...

SYLVIA. Take me home!

JUDY. Where do you live?

SYLVIA & JUDY.
WHO CARES WHERE TINA GETS IT FROM!

JUDY. I know she doesn't get it from me.

SYLVIA. Is your husband talented?

JUDY. I don't think so. Maybe.

SYLVIA. I've heard it said talent often skips a generation.

JUDY. That may be true. I was an adopted child.

SYLVIA. What about your birth parents?

JUDY. I never knew them. But I was raised by two wonderful parents. Dad was a salesman, and Mother? My mother doesn't much like the theatre. She's a theatre critic.

SYLVIA. Lita Encore.

JUDY. You've heard of Mother?

SYLVIA. She's legendary. Your mother's bad reviews closed dozens of plays and countless musicals.

JUDY. She's coming to see Tina's show tonight.

SYLVIA. I must ask her to autograph a copy of her book, "Hooked on Fame! The Dark Truth About Ruth... *DelMarco.*"

[MUSIC NO. 06A "UNDERSCORE"]

JUDY. *(Shivers.)* That name!

SYLVIA. *(Louder.) Ruth DelMarco?*

(JUDY shudders.)

She was a great star of musical theatre. You're too young to have seen her in *Bananas Over Broadway*, but surely you've heard her recording of "I'll Be an Unkie's Muncle." It was a tremendous hit.

[MUSIC NO. 06B "UNDERSCORE"]

JUDY. Strange... I don't recall when it was...or where... Somehow I seem to know that name.

SYLVIA. From your mother's book perhaps?

JUDY. I don't think so. *(Beat.)* Tell me, what's become of... of...

SYLVIA. *(Louder!) Ruth DelMarco?*

(JUDY recoils.)

She's dead. When her last show, *Wings Over Broadway* opened – she was divine as Amelia Earhart, but thanks to Lita's vicious review, the show closed after two performances. Devastated, unable to face anyone, Ruth took her own life.

JUDY. Suddenly the thought of Tina being in show business frightens me.

SYLVIA. I don't understand.

JUDY. What if show people are doomed? Doomed to a lifestyle of booze, pills and heavy meals late at night. That's not the life I want for my child.

> (*JUDY exits to the kitchen,* SYLVIA *follows. Lights fade.*)

> [MUSIC NO. 06C "SCENE CHANGE / UNDERSCORE"]

Scene Six

(Auditorium stage. Three weeks later, afternoon.)

*(**MISS THORN** enters holding a script and dragging on a cardboard palm tree.)*

MISS THORN. Listen up. After the boat sinks in Scene One, all the children who drown, dry off. Girls put on your grass skirts, boys change into your pirate drag. Come on, people. Stop farting around. *(A child giggles.)* Knock it off, Rachel Hobbs. This is a theatre, not some playground. You're not here to have fun. Go music.

[MUSIC NO. 07 "PIPPI SONG (INTRO)"]

*(**LOUISE**, dressed as a shipwrecked Pippi Longstocking, enters and marches to center stage.)*

LOUISE. Coconuts, mangoes, grass huts, and look, the Bora Bora Chez No-No Floatel. This must be Tahiti! And I'm Pippi. Pippi Longstocking! Now that you know who I am, say hello to my best friend. Careful you don't get fleas. My best friend is a dog! Pippi laughs. Come on, Puddles!

*(**TINA** enters. She's wearing her same dress and dog ears.)*

MISS THORN. Where's the rest of your costume?

TINA. Ask Betty Lerman. *(Unhappily takes her place upstage of **LOUISE**.)*

MISS THORN. Keep it moving.

[MUSIC NO. 07A "THE PIPPI SONG"]

And sing out, Louise!

LOUISE.

> HOWDY-DO
> MY NAME IS PIPPI
> P-I-P-P-Y

MISS THORN. Stop! For the last time it's spelled P I P P I.

LOUISE. Oh.

> HOWDY-DO
> MY NAME IS PIPPI
> P-I-P-P-O!
> I BET'CHA THINK THAT I'M A FOOL
> 'CAUSE I DON'T GO TO SCHOOL
> SO I'M NOT SMART, I'M NOT BRIGHT
> THAT'S OKAY, THAT'S ALL GOOD
> ANYONE AS CUTE AS ME
> DON'T NEED A PHD
>
> IN BORA BORA NO ONE'S BORED
> THIS ISLAND'S ALL THE RAGE
> IT'S FULL O' HULA DANCERS
> AND THERE'S NO STINKIN' DRINKIN' AGE
> OUR ADVENTURE'S JUST BEGUN
> AND NOW THAT YOU ALL MET ME
> MEET MY WATER GUN

> *(**LOUISE** takes out a water pistol, squirts the audience twice.)*

MISS THORN. The audience will love it! Makes them part of the show. Do it again!

LOUISE.

> OUR ADVENTURE'S JUST BEGUN
> AND NOW THAT YOU ALL MET ME
> MEET MY WATER GUN

> *(**LOUISE** squirts the audience three times, while **TINA**, who's pulled out a water pistol, squirts **LOUISE**.)*

There was an awful big storm at sea. Our boat sunk and all the passengers drowned. But not me. Puddles saved my life. Way to go, Puddles. Shake. *(Holds out her hand,* **TINA** *doesn't shake.)* You're supposed to shake my hand.

TINA. Look, Louise, you're not the director.

LOUISE. Miss Thorn!

TINA. I'm sorry, I don't think Puddles would shake hands here, okay? Puddles just swam fifty miles to rescue Pippi. I think Puddles would rather lie down.

LOUISE. I'm sorry, I can't act with this.

TINA. You can't act period.

LOUISE. Can too!

TINA. Prove it!

MISS THORN. Tina! Louise! Take it from the Charleston.

[MUSIC NO. 07B "CHARLESTON"]

(They dance a Charleston during the following.)

TINA. The only reason you got the part is because Mommy and Daddy bought it for you.

LOUISE. My parents may open doors for me, but I have to back it up with talent.

TINA. Better get busy. *(They stop dancing.)*

LOUISE. *(To* **MISS THORN**.*)* Do I have to have a dog?

MISS THORN. Yes, Louise. Puddles saves your life.

LOUISE. I forgot.

TINA. Stupid.

LOUISE. *(Rhymes with "Mix-a.")* Shiksa.

TINA. Amateur!

LOUISE. Chorus girl!

TINA. *(Outraged.)* Louise called me a chorus girl!

LOUISE. I did not!

TINA. Asshole!

MISS THORN. That's it! Take ten! Then, Louise, I want to hear the Pippi ballad.

LOUISE. The Pippi what?

MISS THORN. The slow song!

> *(***MISS THORN*** exits, ***LOUISE*** takes out her jump rope and starts jumping, ***TINA*** approaches her.)*

TINA. If you let me play Pippi, I'll be your best friend.

LOUISE. Beat it, Denmark!

TINA. I get it. How much?

LOUISE. I don't want your money. My parents are loaded.

TINA. Please, Louise. I've got to play Pippi!

LOUISE. Better you than me.

TINA. What do you mean?

LOUISE. Do you think I want to be in this show? I think it's embarrassing. But it makes my parents happy. And when Mike and Betty are happy, I'm happy. Got it?

TINA. But I gotta play Pippi!

LOUISE. Too bad! Here. *(Hands* **TINA** *the jump rope.)* I gotta go learn the stupid slow song. *(Exits.)*

TINA. It's called a ballad!

[MUSIC NO. 07C "TO PLAY THIS PART (REPRISE)"]

I ASKED POLITELY
I SAID PLEASE
NOW THERE'S NOTHING LEFT TO DO BUT...

Hey! Wait up, Louise!

> (**TINA** *runs after* **LOUISE**, **MISS THORN** *enters
> and strikes the palm tree.*)

MISS THORN. May I remind the cast the show is tonight,
and if I were me, I wouldn't pay two cents to see this.
(Exits.)

Scene Seven

(Denmark living room. Immediately following.)

(SYLVIA *and* **JUDY** *are having coffee.)*

SYLVIA. I'm sorry, dear, but I'm with Tina on this. What is the point of watching her play a mute dog?

JUDY. Come on, Sylvia. It'll be fun.

SYLVIA. *(Crossing to radio.)* You need to get out more.

JUDY. Come to think of it, I would like to get out of the house. Wouldn't you, Sylvia? Like to get out of the house? Even if I stay at home?

(SYLVIA *switches on the radio.)*

NEWSCASTER. *(Voice-over.)* We interrupt this program with breaking news. One of the students attending Turner Elementary School was discovered with a jump rope around her neck and hanging from the catwalks high above the stage of the school's Vivian Vance Auditorium. The name of the child is being withheld until the parents have been notified. We now return you –

(SYLVIA *turns down the volume.)*

JUDY. Sylvia!

SYLVIA. It was not Tina! Tina is too smart to go playing where she might get hurt, much less killed. *(Phone rings.)* You'll have other children, Judy. You're young and still attractive.

[MUSIC NO. 07D "TINA'S MOTHER (REPRISE)"]

JUDY. *(Answers frantically.)*
HELLO!
YES, THIS IS TINA'S MOTHER!
I HEARD, MRS. WILSON!

SYLVIA. There's more news.

JUDY.
BYE!

> (**JUDY** *slams down the phone,* **SYLVIA** *turns up the volume.*)

NEWSCASTER. *(Voice-over.)* We have been authorized to inform you the victim of the Turner School tragedy was ten-year-old Louise Lerman. Miss Lerman, who was to star tonight in her school production of *Pippi in Tahiti*, was the only child of Mike and Betty Lerman.

> (**SYLVIA** *switches off the radio.*)

JUDY. That poor little girl.

SYLVIA. I know. She probably hasn't had a bite of lunch.

JUDY. I don't know what to do.

SYLVIA. Make her a sandwich.

JUDY. What if she's not ready to handle this?

SYLVIA. *(Checks watch.)* We have eight hours. *(Rushing to door.)* She'll be ready! *(Exits.)*

> (**JUDY** *takes the coffee cups to the kitchen.*)

[MUSIC NO. 07E "UNDERSCORE"]

> (**TINA** *enters, closes the door quietly, and tiptoes toward her room.* **JUDY** *returns.*)

JUDY. Hello, sweetheart.

TINA. *(Freezes, turns, smiles.)* Hello, Mother.

JUDY. You're home early.

TINA. Yes, Mother.

JUDY. *(Pause.)* How was rehearsal?

TINA. Short. Something happened.

JUDY. Come here, sweetheart. Come sit on Mommy's lap.

[MUSIC NO. 07F "UNDERSCORE"]

(**TINA** *puts down her schoolbag, sits in* **JUDY**'s *lap.*)

Tina...

TINA. Mother? What would you give me for a shower of kisses?

JUDY. I'd give you a tub of hugs. *(They embrace.)* Tina...

TINA. Yes, Mother?

JUDY. It might help if you talk to Mommy about what happened today and how you're feeling.

TINA. Okay.

JUDY. *(Pause.)* How are you feeling?

TINA. Hungry. I didn't have lunch.

JUDY. Do you have any questions?

TINA. About?

JUDY. About what happened.

TINA. What happened?

JUDY. To Louise Lerman?

[MUSIC NO. 08 "KISSES AND HUGS"]

TINA. *(Eager to change the subject.)*
I'M SO VERY LUCKY THAT
YOU ARE MY MOTHER
IF I HAD TO CHOOSE
I WOULD NOT CHOOSE ANOTHER
MOMMY AND DADDY

JUDY.
AND TINA MAKES THREE

TINA.
>NO OTHER PARENTS COULD EVER BE
>AS LOVING AS MY PARENTS ARE TO ME

(JUDY tears up.) Why are you crying, Mother?

JUDY. Oh, Tina...
>ACCIDENTS HAPPEN
>THAT NO ONE FORESEES...

TINA. I gotta run lines.

JUDY. What?

TINA. I mean pray for Louise. *(Smiles.)*

JUDY.
>YOU'RE TAKING THIS TRAGEDY WELL
>AND THAT'S GRAND
>BUT IF YOU WANT TO CRY
>OR HOLD MOMMY'S HAND
>OR EVEN STOP SMILING I'D UNDERSTAND

TINA. I'm good.

JUDY. *(Taken aback.)* Good. *(Stands.)* I'll make you a sandwich.

TINA. *(Quickly.)*
>I THINK THAT MY MOMMY
>COULD USE SOME MORE KISSES

JUDY.
>I'LL TRADE THEM FOR HUGS

TOGETHER.
>OH WHAT BLISS THIS IS

>*(They hug. The doorbell chimes, TINA skips off to her room. JUDY opens the door. A dramatic MISS THORN is wearing dark glasses.)*

MISS THORN. *(Sweeps into the room.)* Hello, Mrs. Denmark.

JUDY. Come in, Miss Thorn.

MISS THORN. Do you mind if I smoke?

JUDY. Go right ahead.

MISS THORN. Cigarette?

JUDY. No, thank you.

MISS THORN. Do you have one?

JUDY. I'm afraid I quit.

MISS THORN. Good for you. Cold turkey?

JUDY. I don't think so, but I can look. *(Starts for kitchen.)*

MISS THORN. *(Sighs audibly,* **JUDY** *turns back.)* Please, forgive me. Lord knows I'm trying.

JUDY. We can all be at times.

MISS THORN. *(Removes glasses.)* As you can imagine we're all terribly shaken by this tragedy. The school is collecting money to purchase a memorial fruit and cheese basket for the Lerman family.

JUDY. How thoughtful. Fruit and cheese can be so comforting. The children, did they see Louise? I mean after...

MISS THORN. I'm afraid so. The authorities made it clear no one was to leave the auditorium until they arrived. I told the children not to look up, but *(Chuckles.)* you know how curious they are at that age. *(Beat.)* How's Tina?

JUDY. She's fine. She hasn't said much about it or the show being canceled.

MISS THORN. Mrs. Denmark, Tina's playing Pippi tonight.

JUDY. Excuse me?

MISS THORN. She is the understudy.

JUDY. Yes, but do you think it's a good idea for the children to be singing and dancing so soon after –

MISS THORN. The show is completely sold out. The children have worked so hard, they'd be terribly disappointed, and, frankly, my dear, this is the best work I've ever done.

JUDY. But it's wrong. Shockingly wrong!

MISS THORN. Look, Mrs. D!

[MUSIC NO. 08A "UNDERSCORE"]

I've had it up here with the Pippi people over the damn rights. They're not going to stop me, and neither will you. If Tina does not play Pippi tonight, I shall go to the police!

JUDY. The police?

MISS THORN. To tell them about the Pippi wig.

JUDY. What about the Pippi wig?

MISS THORN. It's missing.

JUDY. Why are you telling me this?

MISS THORN. According to one of our students, Rachel Hobbs, Tina was chasing Louise and grabbing at the wig.

JUDY. Are you suggesting Tina had something to do with what happened?

MISS THORN. Oh, no. The thought never entered my mind.

JUDY. The reporter said it was an accident.

MISS THORN. Of course it was. They're children, they were playing a game, they got over-excited, and one of them got killed…accidentally. According to her understudy.

JUDY. You have the temerity to suggest my child killed for a part in the school show?

MISS THORN. I don't know what temerity means, but it's not just any part, Mrs. Denmark, it's the lead! Now...

[MUSIC NO. 09 "TEACHING THIRD GRADE (REPRISE)"]

I'VE ALTERED THE COSTUME
LOUISE WAS SO BIG

(Indicating Tina's schoolbag.)

YOU'LL HAVE TO COME UP WITH
A RED-BRAIDED WIG
SMILE, MRS. DENMARK
SHE'S GONNA BE GREAT
GOOD GOD, IT'S TWELVE THIRTY
AND THE SHOW STARTS AT EIGHT!

Look on the bright side – now you'll get comps! *(Exits.)*

[MUSIC NO. 09A "UNDERSCORE"]

*(**JUDY** nervously picks up Tina's schoolbag, sits on the sofa, opens the bag, slowly reaches in, and pulls out the Pippi wig.)*

JUDY. *(Whispers.)* Tina?

*(**TINA** bounces in.)*

TINA. Did you call me, Mother?

JUDY. What are you doing with this wig?

TINA. Can we have a ballet bar? Francine Gordon has a ballet bar. Her pop-pop made it with her mee-maw's crutches.

JUDY. Don't change the subject. What is this doing in your schoolbag?

TINA. I saw it laying on the stage after...you know. With everyone screaming and running around, I was afraid it might get stepped on or kicked. So I put it in my bag. Did I do a bad thing.

JUDY. No, Tina. *(Embracing her.)* You did a good thing. Now, we must give the wig to Miss Thorn.

TINA. Why? It's the Pippi wig and I'm playing Pippi.

JUDY. Tina!

TINA. Yes, Mother?

JUDY. Sweetheart, is there something you want to tell Mommy?

TINA. I think you're the nicest mother, and the prettiest mother... Oh, Mother, what would you give me –

JUDY. Tina! Did you have something to do with what happened to Louise?

TINA. What happened? Remind me.

JUDY. You did it, didn't you.

TINA. What did I do, didn't I?

JUDY. You killed Louise Lerman!

TINA. And...?

JUDY. You killed Louise Lerman for a part in a show?

TINA. Not just any part, Mother. The lead!

JUDY. Oh, my god! Tina, you have to tell me everything. Start at the beginning and tell me the whole story.

TINA. Okay. There's a big boat onstage and it's sinking!

JUDY. Not the show. Forget the show. Tell me about Louise.

TINA. We got to rehearsal.

JUDY. Go on.

TINA. We changed clothes.

JUDY. Go on.

TINA. We ran scene two.

JUDY. Go on.

TINA. Louise hung herself.

JUDY. Back up.

TINA. I told Louise I just had to play Pippi. She said too bad, so I chased her. I chased her up onto the catwalks. I think it was after she said, "Over my dead body!" is when I wrapped the jump rope around her neck and pushed her over the side.

[MUSIC NO. 09B "UNDERSCORE"]

JUDY. Oh, Tina! Tina! Look at me, Tina. You did a terrible thing.

TINA. Yes, Mother.

JUDY. You killed that little girl.

TINA. Yes, Mother.

JUDY. Do you know what this means?

TINA. It means I'm playing Pippi. *(Picks up the wig.)*

JUDY. I think someone needs to go to her room!

TINA. But Mommy, the show!

JUDY. *(Grabs wig.)* Never mind the show! Go to your room! You're punished!

> (**TINA** *runs off.* **SYLVIA** *enters, carrying a shopping bag.* **JUDY** *frantically hides the wig.)*

SYLVIA. Is she ready? Is everything laid out? Makeup box, ballet shoes, her new opening night party dress?

JUDY. What...? What new dress?

SYLVIA. This one! *(Holds up an over-the-top pageant dress.)*

JUDY. Please, Sylvia. Not now!

[MUSIC NO. 10 "TALENT (REPRISE 1)"]

SYLVIA.
SHE'LL LOOK EVERY INCH THE STAR
IN WHAT I BOUGHT HER
NOW IF SHE JUST REMEMBERS
ALL I'VE TAUGHT HER...
TONIGHT WE LAUNCH A NEW CAREER
IT WON'T BE LONG BEFORE THEY CHEER
AND GIVE HER A STANDING OVATION
FIRST COMES FORTUNE THEN COMES FAME
THEN THE TINA DOLL AND THE TINA GAME
SHE'S GOING TO BECOME A CORPORATION!

JUDY. Stop it, Sylvia! *(Doubles over in pain.)* What am I going to do?

SYLVIA. What's the matter, dear? *(Catches on.)* Oh. Are you having your ladies?

> *(Doorbell chimes.)*

JUDY. That will be Mother.

[MUSIC NO. 10A "UNDERSCORE"]

> *(**JUDY** crosses to the door, opens it. **LITA ENCORE** enters, holding a modest bouquet of flowers.)*

LITA. Where's my granddaughter?

JUDY. She's being punished.

LITA. Tina? Punished? I must be in the wrong house! *(Bursts out laughing.)* Here. *(Tosses bouquet to **JUDY**, sees **SYLVIA**.)* Hello.

JUDY. Mother, this is Tina's manager, Sylvia St. Croix.

> *(**TINA** runs on.)*

TINA. Grandmother!

LITA. Darling! Have you been naughty?

TINA. Have you?

LITA. *(To audience.)* I love this kid.

TINA. How much?

LITA. This much. *(Makes an "inch" with her fingers.)*

TINA. More!

LITA. This much! *(Arms wide.)*

TINA. More!

LITA. Oh. *(Grabs bouquet from* JUDY, *gives it to* TINA.*)* Here.

TINA. Look, Sylvia.

SYLVIA. Mine are in the car. Much bigger.

TINA. Here. *(Returns bouquet to* LITA.*)*

JUDY. Back to your room, young lady!

LITA. *(Disappointed.)* Awww!

JUDY. Mother, you can play with Tina later.

SYLVIA. Come along, Tina. *(Starts for bedroom.)* You can try on your new dress, and we still have work to do on the Pippi ballad. *(Exits.)*

TINA. *(To* LITA.*)* A ballad is a slow song.

LITA. Darling, I remember you when you were this big. *(Holds hand waist-high.)*

TINA. And I remember you when you were sober! *(Grabs bouquet from* LITA, *exits.)*

JUDY. *(Crossing to bar.)* Would you like a drink?

LITA. Are you having one?

JUDY. Oh, yes. Yes, indeed. *(Pours two drinks.)*

LITA. Now, what's this twaddle about my granddaughter being punished?

JUDY. Mother, you know Frederick and I have always –

LITA. Wait. Who?

JUDY. Frederick. My husband. We've always encouraged Tina –

LITA. Wait. You're married?

JUDY. *(Hands* **LITA** *a drink,* **LITA** *downs it.)* Mother, I don't want Tina to perform! I don't want her to ever set foot on a stage again. That goes for tonight.

LITA. Darling, if you think I've come all this way to sit through some farchadat *[fa-cocked-a]* Pippi musical my granddaughter isn't performing in, you're out of your mind.

JUDY. But Mother –

LITA. Honey…

[MUSIC NO. 11 "I HATE MUSICALS!"]

WHEN I GO TO THE THEATRE
I HOPE IT'S A PLAY
WITH NO SINGING AND DANCING
TO GET IN THE WAY
THEATRE IS LANGUAGE
AND THAT SHOULD BE ALL
MUSIC BELONGS AT THE CARNEGIE HALL
NOT A REASON ON EARTH
AS FAR AS I KNOW
TO WRITE, MOUNT, AND OPEN
A MUSICAL SHOW

(She goes for another refill.)

Darling, I've been a theatre critic for a hundred years and it's always the same.

THE STORY IS MOVING
CHOCK-FULL OF SUSPENSE
THE PLOT TAKES A TWIST
THE MOOD IS INTENSE
THEN SOMEONE SINGS A SONG LIKE THIS!
IT DOESN'T MAKE SENSE
I HATE MUSICALS!

GANGS DON'T LOOK TOUGH
WHEN THEY TWIRL AND THEY SNAP
MY GORGE STARTS TO RISE
IF A NUN STARTS TO TAP
AND WOULDN'T YOU JUST LOVE
TO SLAP MARIA VON TRAPP?

I'll tell you how to solve a problem like Maria. "Hey, Rolf! *(Points.)* She's over there!"

I HATE MUSICALS!

REVIVALS ARE IRRELEVANT DESPITE REDESIGN
MUSICALS DO NOT AGE WELL
LIKE BLUE CHEESE AND WINE
WITHOUT A PLOT THOSE JUKEBOX SHOWS
ARE LIGHT AS A FEATHER
WITH SCORES OF OLD RECYCLED SONGS
COBBLED TOGETHER

FOR ME TO REVIEW ONE
DEMANDS ALCOHOL
THE UPSHOT IS I SHOW UP LATE...
IF I SHOW UP AT ALL
THERE'S ROWS OF THOSE
WHO FIND THESE SHOWS
DELIGHTFUL, NOT ME
TO ME THEY'RE DEBRIS
AND THREE HOURS LONG
I HATE MUSICALS
BUT NOT AS MUCH AS I HATE...
THIS SONG!

*(**LITA** crosses to **JUDY**. The music starts up, signaling her encore.)*

THEY CAN HOLD YOU HOSTAGE
FOR AS LONG AS THEY WANT
OH BOY, HERE COMES ANOTHER VERSE
FROM SOME WASHED-UP CU...OW
GIVE ME ARTHUR MILLER, BECKETT
CHEKHOV OR MAMET
AND JESUS WAS A SAVIOR
NOT A SUPERSTAR GODDAMN IT!

SO KEEP YOUR CHORUS LINES
OF GYPSYS AND MAMES
I'D RATHER SEE A FLICK
OR BOWL A FEW FRAMES
NO MATTER WHO IS STARRING
I'M NEVER ENTICED
IT'S WAY OVER-PRICED
EVEN THOUGH I DON'T PAY
I HATE MUSICALS
BUT I FEAR THEY'RE HERE TO STAY
YES, I HATE MUSICALS
BUT NOT AS MUCH AS
I HATE BALLET!

JUDY. Much as I'd love to hear another chorus, there's something I need to ask you. Who are my real parents?

*(**SYLVIA** enters.)*

SYLVIA. Tina's having her bath. Judy, I've arranged for a photographer, so wear something gorgeous. They may do a mother-daughter spread.

JUDY. It's a school show, Sylvia.

SYLVIA. It's the start of her career.

JUDY. I'm not sure I want her to have a career.

SYLVIA. I'm not sure you have a choice. Show business is in that child's blood.

LITA. Thank you, I'd love another drink. *(Goes to bar for a refill.)*

JUDY. I've made up my mind. No more show business.

SYLVIA. What about what Tina wants?

JUDY. Tina? Tina will be happier in the Brownies.

SYLVIA. No!

[MUSIC NO. 11A "UNDERSCORE"]

She'll die in the Brownies! *(Beat.)* Judy, I think you do want this...but you're afraid.

JUDY. Afraid?

SYLVIA. Of how desperately you want it. But not for Tina... for yourself!

LITA. I thought this was a comedy? It's a melodrama?

JUDY. *(To* SYLVIA.*)* What are you saying?

LITA. I thought this was a comedy. Is my mic not on?

SYLVIA. Admit it. It's you who wants to be a star!

JUDY. What?

SYLVIA. You're jealous of your daughter's talent.

JUDY. I am deliriously happy leading a normal, ordinary life. And so too will my daughter.

[MUSIC NO. 11B "UNDERSCORE"]

SYLVIA. "A normal life was not possible. Not for a desperate woman who depended on strangers loving her night after night in a dark theatre." I'm quoting you, Encore. It's a passage from your book, *Hooked on Fame! The Dark Truth About Ruth...DelMarco.*

[MUSIC NO. 11C "UNDERSCORE"]

JUDY. *(Recoils.)* That name!

LITA. I don't deny she had talent, but the woman was insane. Imagine killing yourself over a bad review.

SYLVIA. A review written by Lita Encore.

LITA. Whoops.

SYLVIA. Your review closed her show. But for your vicious words, Ruth DelMarco would still be alive.

LITA. Perhaps she is.

SYLVIA. Excuse me?

LITA. They never found her body, just those big footprints in the sand and a suicide note, "Good-bye cruel world." Three words. Two of which were misspelled. And as far as killing Ruth DelMarco –

SYLVIA. Do you deny that –

LITA. Three years ago Ruth DelMarco was spotted doing *I Do, I Do* in Bucks County!

SYLVIA. That's just a rumor.

LITA. Perhaps. But they never found her body.

SYLVIA. Or her child.

[MUSIC NO. 11D "UNDERSCORE"]

JUDY. There was a child?

LITA. Another rumor.

JUDY. Ruth DelMarco had a child?

SYLVIA. A little girl, I believe.

[MUSIC NO. 11E "UNDERSCORE"]

LITA. Who wants lunch?

TINA. *(Offstage.)* Sylvia!

SYLVIA. Coming, Tina.

LITA. Mommy's starving.

SYLVIA. *(Exiting.)* She kept it quiet, of course. I don't think anyone knew who the father was. *(Exits.)*

JUDY. Oh, Mother.

SYLVIA. *(Pokes her head in.)* Bob Fosse. But you didn't hear it from me. *(Disappears.)*

JUDY. I want my child to be happy.

LITA. She is happy.

JUDY. I want her to be normal.

LITA. She is happy.

JUDY. Mother?

LITA. Yes, dear?

JUDY. Who am I?

LITA. You're my daughter and I love you very much. Let's eat.

JUDY. Where do I come from?

LITA. The Judy department at Sears!

JUDY. Who are my real parents?

LITA. Please, Ginger!

[MUSIC NO. 11F "UNDERSCORE"]

JUDY. Ginger?

LITA. I mean Judy.

JUDY. You called me…Ginger.

[MUSIC NO. 11G "UNDERSCORE"]

LITA. I knew one day God would punish me for panning *Fiddler*. Come, we'll have a quiet lunch, just the two of us and afterwards a long talk. Please. We need time.

JUDY. I understand.

LITA. You're Ruth DelMarco's child!

[MUSIC NO. 11H "UNDERSCORE"]

JUDY. *(Collapses.)* Oh my god!

LITA. You tore it out of me!

JUDY. Are you saying –

LITA. I know what you're thinking and it's not true!

JUDY. *(Staggers around.)* I'm talented!

LITA. No!

JUDY. God help me, I'm talented!

LITA. Darling, you're not!

JUDY. It's all my fault! Her talent, her drive –

LITA. Tell me what you want?

JUDY. Her pathological need to be famous!

LITA. Chinese or Italian?

JUDY. All this time, all this talent...in me! *(Cringes.)* Oh, I feel so cheap and dirty. How did this happen?

[MUSIC CUE NO. 11I "UNDERSCORE"]

LITA. I heard Ruth had a child. When she disappeared, I came looking and I found the most beautiful little girl. You. Alone, frightened, chained to your mother's dressing room table. Oh, Judy –

[MUSIC NO. 11J "UNDERSCORE"]

JUDY. No! My name is Ginger DelMarco!

[MUSIC NO. 11K "UNDERSCORE"]

LITA. You are my daughter. I raised you ever since you were two years old.

JUDY. *(Wilts into* **LITA**'s *arms.)* Oh, Mother.

LITA. Okay, seven, what's the difference? You were an ordinary child.

JUDY. Was I, Mother? Was I?

LITA. Yes and you're still nothing special.

JUDY. How can you be sure?

LITA. I know average when I see it. You grew up beautifully. You married what's his name, Kenneth.

JUDY. Frederick.

LITA. Yeah, him, and together you gave birth to –

TINA. *(Skips onstage, singing.)*
HOWDY-DO
MY NAME IS PIPPI
P-I-P-P-I *(Plops down.)*

LITA. You must take care of your daughter.

JUDY. Mother, she...

LITA. She needs you.

SYLVIA. *(Offstage.)* Tina! Get back here!

JUDY. She...she...

LITA. She needs you now more than ever! *(Beat.)* Darling, I am so glad we finally had this little chat. *(Crosses to front door.)* I feel so much better, don't you?

> *(***JUDY*** stares into space.)*

I'll meet you at the theatre. Break a leg, Tina! And don't forget, you owe me, kiddo. Because as much as Grandmama loves you...

[MUSIC NO. 11L "I HATE MUSICALS! (REPRISE)"]

I HATE MUSICALS!

(LITA exits as SYLVIA enters. JUDY hasn't moved.)

SYLVIA. Okay, Tina! The Pippi ballad from the top.

TINA. I'm tired, Sylvia.

SYLVIA. Come on, come on, it's almost there.

TINA. Okay. *(Sings childishly.)*
WHEN I WAS A LITTLE GIRL
A LITTLE –

SYLVIA. No! It's too cute. It needs weight. Again.

TINA. *(Sings overly dramatically.)*
WHEN I WAS A LITTLE –

SYLVIA. No tears, damn it! What did I teach you? *(Cueing her.)* If you cry...

TINA. If I cry, the audience won't.

SYLVIA. Precisely. Start again!

TINA. No.

SYLVIA. Tina!

TINA. I'm tired and I'm hungry.

SYLVIA. You're a quitter.

TINA. It's a lousy song anyway.

SYLVIA. There are no lousy songs. Only lazy singers! Here. I'll show you how it's done.

[MUSIC NO. 12 "ANGEL MOM (SYLVIA)"]

(As SYLVIA prepares to perform, JUDY slowly shifts her gaze to watch her. SYLVIA's performance quickly becomes too theatrical, over the top.)

WHEN I WAS A LITTLE GIRL
A LITTLE GIRL OF SEVEN
MY MOMMY UNEXPECTEDLY
WENT ON A TRIP TO HEAVEN
AND DADDY DEAR WOULD KISS MY TEAR
WHEN I WOULD START TO CRY

JUDY. *(Suddenly, as if possessed.)* It's too big, Sylvia! *(Looks around to see where the voice came from.)*

SYLVIA. I beg your pardon?

JUDY. *(Slowly, intuitively.)* It's...too big. You want the audience to come to you. *(Mystified by her own words.)*

SYLVIA. Excuse me, Judy Denmark, but what would you possibly know about it?

JUDY. *(Slowly gaining confidence.)* I know enough to see you're pushing for results. You're not in the moment. You have no subtext. You don't know the first thing about Pippi Longstocking. *(Self-assured.)* You're not even acting. I see what you're doing.

SYLVIA. You wouldn't dare.

JUDY. *(In her face.)* You're indicating!

> (**SYLVIA** *indicates being mortified, turns away, staggers upstage.*)

TINA. Mama? Will you show me how it's done?

[MUSIC NO. 12A "ANGEL MOM (JUDY)"]

> (**JUDY** *slowly removes her apron and tosses it aside. Just as she's about to sing, she falters.*)

JUDY. I can't. *(Turns away.)*

SYLVIA. *(Turns to her.)* Yes. You can.

JUDY. *(Instantly turns back, sings, remaining perfectly still.)*

WHEN I WAS A LITTLE GIRL
A LITTLE GIRL OF SEVEN
MY MOMMY UNEXPECTEDLY
WENT ON A TRIP TO HEAVEN
AND DADDY DEAR WOULD KISS MY TEAR
WHEN I WOULD START TO CRY
AND SAY THOUGH MOMMY'S DEAD
SHE'S OVERHEAD
AN ANGEL IN THE SKY

(Slowly, her arms start moving. She looks at her hands in wonder.)

Mama? *(Looks to heaven.)* M...M...Mama?

(Remaining in place, she sings, gesturing expressively with her arms and hands.)

NOW WHEN I LAY ME DOWN TO SLEEP
I DON'T TURN OFF THE LIGHT
SO MOM CAN FIND ME WHEN SHE COMES
TO KISS MY CHEEK GOOD NIGHT
OF COURSE I RAISE MY WINDOW NOW
BEFORE I GET IN BED
I WOULDN'T WANT MY ANGEL MOM
TO BANG HER ANGEL HEAD

(She owns it.) I'm a talented girl, Mama!

(Takes the stage with confidence.)

YOU MAY SAY I'M MOTHER-LESS
BUT I MUST DISAGREE
I LIVE FOR MY MOTHER
AND MY MOTHER LIVES IN ME
NOW EVERYTHING I'LL EVER DO
AND EVERYTHING I'LL BE
I'LL BE BECAUSE OF MOMMY DEAR
MY MOTHER LIVES IN ME!

Tina! Take the third chorus! *(Coaching her brusquely.)*

TINA.
>YOU MAY SAY I'M MOTHER-LESS
>BUT I MUST DISAGREE

JUDY. Arms!

TINA. *(Throws arms open.)*
>I LIVE FOR MY MOTHER
>AND MY MOTHER LIVES IN ME

JUDY. Smile, baby!

>*(**SYLVIA** watches with tears in her eyes as mother and daughter perform side by side, the mirror image of one another.)*

JUDY & TINA.
>NOW EVERYTHING I EVER DO
>AND EVERYTHING I'LL BE
>I'LL BE BECAUSE OF MOMMY DEAR
>MOMMY'S HERE!
>MY MOTHER LIVES IN ME!

>*(Blackout.)*

ACT II

(Prologue.)

JUDY. *(Voice-over.)* Dear Frederick. Our little girl has committed an unspeakable crime...so I turned her in. Perhaps it was a mistake allowing Sylvia to handle her defense.

(Lights up on **SYLVIA.***)*

SYLVIA. Ladies and gentlemen of the jury, my heart goes out to Mike and Betty Lerman as they face the unimaginable grief of losing their only child. Still, they were spared the humiliation of being trapped in an audience, pretending to enjoy their untalented kid stumbling around the stage for two and a half hours. What happened to Louise Lerman was tragic indeed, but it was an accident that Tina Denmark is as innocent of causing as she was sensational as Pippi Longstocking!

(Polite applause.)

JUDGE. *(Voice-over.)* Tina Denmark, I hereby sentence you to serve eight years at the Daisy Clover School for Psychopathic Ingenues. *(Gavel bangs.)* Break a leg.

[MUSIC NO. 13 "ACT II PROLOGUE"]

SYLVIA. *(To audience.)* Talent! Inherited and unstoppable, dragging generation after generation into the spotlight. Remember Judy Denmark? She was no match for the emerging ego-driven barracuda called Ginger

57

DelMarco, and slowly she disappeared until sadly, Judy Denmark was no more.

TONY PRESENTER. *(Voice-over.)* This year's Tony Award for Leading Actress in a Musical goes to Ginger DelMarco for *Pardon My Wind*!

(Cheering and applause.)

SYLVIA. A lot can happen in one year. If a picture is worth a thousand words, imagine what you can learn from an entire Second Act! Meet Ginger DelMarco!

Scene Eight

(Ginger DelMarco's New York penthouse. One year later.)

[MUSIC NO. 13A "NYC MUSIC"]

*(***GINGER DELMARCO*** sweeps onstage wearing a kimono and brandishing a long cigarette holder, holding a cigarette she never lights. She strikes a glamorous, non-smiling pose, then sprawls across her designer sofa.)*

SYLVIA. Ginger DelMarco, a born-again talent who doesn't give a damn about baking cookies or making a bed.

(The phone rings, **GINGER** *makes a point of ignoring it.)*

A star package surrounded by agents, managers, hairdressers, and...

EVE. *(Enters, poses, smiles.)* I'll get it. *(Phone rings.)*

SYLVIA. Her devoted personal assistant...

EVE. *(Answers phone.)* This is Eve.

SYLVIA. Eve.

[MUSIC NO. 13B "NYC MUSIC (CONT.)"]

A clutching, clawing Broadway wannabe clinging oh so desperately to the hem of success.

EVE. Sorry, Miss DelMarco never comes to the phone. *(Crossing to* **GINGER***, phone in hand.)* You'll have to wait until she calls you. *(Holds receiver out for* **GINGER** *to speak into.)*

GINGER. Bye-bye.

(GINGER and EVE laugh until GINGER abruptly cuts it off and glides offstage. EVE hangs up, pretends to tidy up the apartment.)

SYLVIA. It was a Tuesday morning. I had breakfast at Lindy's. The usual, an order of toast and the bottomless daiquiri, then headed straight to Ginger's apartment. *(Exits.)*

[MUSIC NO. 14 "PENTHOUSE APARTMENT"]

EVE.
> THAT'S PENTHOUSE APARTMENT
> A VIEW OF THE PARK, OH
> LIFE IS A LARK, OH
> FOR GINGER DELMARC-O
> SHE'S ROLLING IN DOUGH, OH
> LAST WEEK DOWN IN SO-HO
> SHE PICKED UP A RENOIR
> TO GO WITH HER VAN GOGH
>
> HEY, LOOK AT ME, OH
> A KID FROM TOLE-DO!
> LIVIN' THE HIGH LIFE
> I WISH IT WERE MY LIFE
> BEING PERSISTENT
> I BECAME HER ASSISTANT
> I SOAK UP HER GLAMOUR
> AND SOMETIMES I AM HER!
>
> I PUT ON HER UNDIES
> HER PERFUME AND JEWELS
> SLIP INTO HER NIGHTIES
> AND SLAP ON HER MULES
> I GUZZLE HER LIQUOR
> I EAT ALL HER FOOD
> I CUDDLE HER TONY
> WHEN I'M IN THE NUDE
> I SPRAWL ON HER BED

I READ ALL HER MAIL
I STUDY HER MOVEMENTS
EVERY DETAIL
SO EDGY AND WOUND-UP
SHE'S BOUND TO COLLAPSE
I'LL BE WAITIN' IN THE WINGS
WHEN GINGER SNAPS!

I PICK UP HER TISSUES
WHEN SHE HAS THE FLU, 'CHOO!
WHEN IT'S OFF TO THE BEACH
I BRAZILIAN HER HOOHOO
I COOK AND CLEAN
I WASH AND SEW
I WALK THE DOG
AND YEAH, I KNOW...
I'M A GLORIFIED MAID
BUT I'M HAVING THE TIME OF *HER* LIFE
AND GETTIN' PAID

> *(**EVE** does faux straightening up, before losing it.)*

I WANT A PENTHOUSE APARTMENT!
LIKE GINGER DELMARC-OH, YEAH!

I'll get it.

> *(Doorbell chimes. **EVE** never acknowledges jumping the doorbell cues.)*

[MUSIC NO. 14A]

> *(**EVE** crosses to the door, opens it. **SYLVIA**, Pippi wig in hand, breezes past **EVE** and heads for the bar.)*

How did you get past the doorman?

SYLVIA. Easy. I didn't wake him up. *(Plops wig on tall bottle, pours a drink.)* Is she here?

EVE. You know Miss DelMarco never receives visitors. You'll have to wait until she calls on you. Bye-bye.

SYLVIA. So this is the thanks I get for everything I've done for her. Now that she's a star she thinks she doesn't need me anymore. Well, I don't need you, Miss Broadway Star! Miss I-Did-It-All-By-Myself. *(Yells.)* Miss Thanks-A-Lot-And-Out-With-The-Garbage!

> (**GINGER** *sweeps in, holding her cigarette holder, a cocktail dress, and a section of newspaper.*)

EVE. Lower your voice.

GINGER. I got me a better idea. Ferme la bouche.

EVE. Yeah, ferme la bouche.

SYLVIA. In English?

GINGER & EVE. Shut your pie hole!

GINGER. Eve.

EVE. Yes, Miss DelMarco?

GINGER. I told you to speak French, damn it!

EVE. Ouí, Miss DelMarco?

GINGER. Here! *(Flings dress at her.)* I got a stain on this.

EVE. Merde!

GINGER. No, I think it's clam sauce.

EVE. Ouí, Miss DelMarco.

SYLVIA. *We* have to talk.

GINGER. Call my press agent.

SYLVIA. I am your press agent.

GINGER. Not anymore, you're not. Have you seen today's paper? *(Flings newspaper at* **EVE.***)* Read it.

EVE. "With rave reviews and a Tony Award, Ginger DelMarco remains a mystery. Though she claims to be the love child of the infamous Ruth DelMarco, the big question isn't who she is or where she's from. It's why is she wasting her time doing a musical?"

SYLVIA. That's just your mother being a bore.

GINGER. She's not my mother, she hates musicals, and I'm the toast of Broadway.

SYLVIA. Toast? Don't you mean Danish?

[MUSIC NO. 14B]

EVE & GINGER. Danish?

SYLVIA. As in Denmark?

[MUSIC NO. 14C]

EVE & GINGER. Denmark?

SYLVIA. As in Judy Denmark?

[MUSIC NO. 14D]

GINGER. *(Whispers.)* Do something, Eve.

EVE. *(Hisses in* **SYLVIA***'s ear with a Cockney accent.)* Don't scratch your scabs or they'll never get any better!

GINGER. She's nuts, but I don't pay her much.

SYLVIA. Afraid I'll talk? Tell the world you're a married housewife with a kid in reform school.

GINGER. Me? Married and with a child? Ridiculous! A packed house is all the family I need! Eve, why don't you take our guest to the kitchen and fix her a snack.

EVE. *(Exiting.)* Come on, Sylvia. I've got sushi in the oven.

    *(***SYLVIA*** doesn't budge.)*

GINGER. I've never seen you turn down food.

SYLVIA. We have to talk.

GINGER. All right. *(Beat.)* But after my song.

> *(**SYLVIA** exits. When nothing happens, she cues the music.)*

Boys? *(Removes kimono.)*

[MUSIC NO. 15 "IT CAN NEVER BE THAT WAY AGAIN"]

ONCE LIFE WAS SIMPLE
AND ENTRES NOUS
I WAS AN ORDINARY NOTHING

> *(To audience member.)*

JUST LIKE YOU
A HO HUM COLORLESS ROUTINE
MY LIFE OF LAUNDRY AND CAFFEINE
I WAS A MOTHER AND A HOUSEWIFE
WAY BACK WHEN
IT WILL NEVER BE THAT WAY AGAIN

I LOST THE APRON
I FOUND MY VOICE
WHEN YOU'RE BORN TO ENTERTAIN
YOU HAVE NO CHOICE
AS SOMEONE BLESSED WITH GREAT SUCCESS
I KNOW I MUST NOT ACQUIESCE
IF TEMPTED TO INDULGE
A HOUSEWIFE YEN
IT WILL NEVER BE THAT WAY AGAIN

The truth is, last night – and this is strictly between us, I was lying in bed fighting an urge to defrost my freezer. *(Beat.)* There's more. I've had this crazy notion of giving up a sold-out matinee to sit alone and listen to the warm hum of a vacuum cleaner. *(Finds hidden stash of Lemon Pledge.)* Sometimes all I can think about is that sweet metallic screechy sound it makes when you set up an ironing board. *(Sprays Pledge on surface.)* Don't get me wrong. I'm not saying I want to iron. I don't! I can't! I'm a star! *(Snorts Pledge off surface.)*

NOW PEOPLE LOVE ME
FROM HELL TO MAINE
ALL I WANT IS ALL OF YOU
AND EXPENSIVE CHAMPAGNE
ONCE LONG AGO AND FAR AWAY
BEFORE THIS BROAD WAS ON BROADWAY
I HAD A BROOM, NOT JUST AN EGO
WAY BACK WHEN
NOW I STAR IN BROADWAY SHOWS
'CAUSE IN MY VEINS THE TALENT FLOWS

This time I'm doing it for me, Mama!

IT WILL NEVER BE THAT WAY AGAIN!

> *(She runs her finger over the Pledge residue, rubs it on her gums, spots the Pippi wig, and screams.)*

[MUSIC NO. 15A "UNDERSCORE"]

Auuggghh! *(Holds up wig.)* What the hell?

> *(**SYLVIA** enters.)*

SYLVIA. Something to remind you.

GINGER. Of what?

SYLVIA. She'll be back. Not for years, but one day Tina will knock on your door. What will you do then?

GINGER. Pretend I'm not home?

SYLVIA. As a young woman, she'll need someone to guide her.

GINGER. Someone. But not you. Tina and I were doing just fine before you showed up. Now look where she is. Locked away with the criminally talented.

SYLVIA. Tina's strong. And when she's done her time she'll be ready for her career. One, I dare say, as big as...

GINGER. Ginger DelMarco?

SYLVIA. I've done everything for you and you appreciate nothing. Without me there'd be no Ginger DelMarco!

GINGER. *(Suddenly sweet.)* I'm sorry, darling. I know I can be a bit much sometimes.

SYLVIA. And...?

GINGER. And I appreciate all you've done for me. I do.

SYLVIA. And...?

GINGER. Okay, I'm sorry I forget to mention your name when I won the Tony! *(Beat.)* Wait! *(Gets Tony Award, makes speech.)* This award isn't mine alone. I share it with great appreciation for someone who knows me perhaps better than I know myself. Miss Sylvia St. Croix. *(Hands* **SYLVIA** *the Tony, kisses both cheeks.)*

SYLVIA. You're going to make me cry.

GINGER. Thank you, Sylvia. Thank you.

SYLVIA. Oh, Ginger, think of all the wonderful things we'll do together.

GINGER. So many wonderful things. Only not together.

SYLVIA. Here. *(Hands back Tony.)*

GINGER. Sylvia, I'm grateful. I am. *(Beat.)* The thing is I... I...don't know how to say this. *(Deep breath.)* I've outgrown you. I do know how to say it!

SYLVIA. You're tired. We'll have lunch before the matinee and talk.

GINGER. Darling, as much as I don't want to, I can't. I'm flying to the coast to shoot a screen test.

SYLVIA. Movies! So the Broadway star is ditching Broadway.

GINGER. I'll be back for Tuesday night's performance.

SYLVIA. Well, you can't go! You agreed to do the matinee, or has it slipped your mind your understudy has a broken jaw?

GINGER. Yeah, well she started it.

SYLVIA. Don't worry. I'll reschedule your screen test.

GINGER. No, Sylvia.

SYLVIA. I'll do the matinee.

GINGER. Please, Sylvia.

SYLVIA. I'll regrout the master bathroom.

GINGER. Let me go, Sylvia.

SYLVIA. I can't!

GINGER. You've got to let me go! I'll give you anything you want. A new car, a mink coat, an acting school for… oh, I don't know, whoever wants to go to your acting school.

[MUSIC NO. 16 "I WANT THE GIRL"]

SYLVIA.
    YOU SAY THAT I CAN HAVE ANYTHING
    THAT I WANT?

GINGER. Name it.

SYLVIA.
    I WANT THE GIRL.
    YOU SAY YOU WILL PAY ANY PRICE?
    MAY I BE BLUNT?
    I WANT THE GIRL
    LOOK AROUND
    LOOK WHAT I'VE MADE HERE
    I'VE DONE EVERYTHING FOR YOU
    I'M NOT CUTTING OUT

TILL I'M PAID, DEAR
SO SAVE YOUR BEHAVIOR
IT'S MUCH TOO ABUSIVE
I WANT THE GIRL
AND I WANT AN EXCLUSIVE

GINGER. I know this rotten business inside and out, and I will not allow my child anywhere near it.

SYLVIA. Afraid of the competition?

GINGER. Goodbye, Sylvia. *(Exits.)*

SYLVIA.
SHE THINKS THAT SHE CAN
TOSS ME ASIDE
SHE'S GOT HER NERVE
I'LL GET THE GIRL
SO HOPELESSLY WRAPPED UP
IN HER LIFE

(Calls offstage:)

YOU DON'T DESERVE
THAT PRECIOUS GIRL!

TRUE, HER REVIEWS MAY BE GLOWING
THE CRITICS' DARLING, THEY SAY
WELL, DARLING YOUR EGO IS SHOWING
TODAY'S HOT TAMALE
TOMORROW GROWS COLDER
THE FUTURE IS HERE, DEAR
LOOK OVER YOUR SHOULDER
I'M GONNA TAKE HER
AND I'M GONNA MAKE HER
A BIGGER STAR
A BRIGHTER STAR THAN YOU!

STAND BACK!
SHE'S HITTIN' THE HEIGHTS

THAT GORGEOUS FACE
THOSE GOLDEN CURLS
I SEE A BLAZING THEATRE MARQUEE
MY NAME IN LIGHTS...
I MEAN THE GIRL'S

GINGER, A WORD OF ADVICE, DEAR
DON'T LOSE YOUR SOUL TO SUCCESS
FAME IS A FOOL'S PARADISE, DEAR
YOU ARE WHO YOU ARE
ALTHOUGH YOU WIN PRIZES
I WOULDN'T BURN BRIDGES
LIFE'S FULL OF SURPRISES

TINA, I'LL BE HERE
I'M WAITING FOR YOU, DEAR
TO FINISH WHAT WE
STARTED OUT TO DO
YOU WAIT AND SEE
AND ALL THAT I DID

ALL THAT I DO
IS FOR GINGER AND YOU
IT ISN'T FOR ME
NOT FOR ME
NOT FOR ME
FOR ME!
FOR ME!
NOT FOR ME!

*(**GINGER** and **EVE** enter, clapping slowly.)*

GINGER. Are we done?

SYLVIA. We are.

GINGER. Do we want to freshen up?

SYLVIA. We do.

EVE. There's a gas station on the corner.

SYLVIA. I'm not leaving until we have a deal. Now if you'll excuse me, I'll be in the guest room having a lie-down. *(Exits.)*

GINGER. Try not to get makeup all over my new pillow shams.

EVE. I'll get it. *(Crossing to door.)*

> *(Doorbell chimes,* **EVE** *opens the door.)*

> **[MUSIC NO. 16A "TINA'S ENTRANCE"]**

> *(***GINGER** *stares in disbelief as* **TINA** *enters wearing a prison-striped version of her Act I dress and carrying a suitcase. She appears more grown-up. Walking slowly, she looks around, sets down the suitcase. Note: The suitcase must be set down close to where Sylvia will collapse later on.)*

GINGER. Quelle surprise! I didn't expect to see you for at least another seven years.

TINA. I got early parole. I played Annie and her dog, Sandy, in the same production. Good behavior, great reviews, and here I am.

GINGER. Eve, I'd like you to meet my...my... It's on the tip of my tongue. My...

TINA. Daughter.

GINGER. Yes. Say hello to my daughter... *(Forgets her name.)* My daughter...

TINA. Tina.

EVE. Nice to meet you. I've heard absolutely nothing about you. *(Beat.)* Hold the phone! Did you say Tina? As in Tina Denmark? *(Irish accent.)* Ain't ya the dame what killed the wee Lerman lassie for a part in a play?

GINGER. Not just any part. The lead!

EVE. How'd ya do it?

GINGER. She hung her with a jump rope. *(To* **TINA.***)* Remember that? I was so angry with you. Now there's a dozen actresses I'd like to hang with a jump rope. *(Laughs.)*

EVE. I can think of one. *(Imitates* **GINGER***'s laugh.)*

GINGER. Eve? Why don't you take Puddles for his afternoon walkie?

EVE. It's the leash I can do!

[MUSIC NO. 16B "UNDERSCORE"]

Vive le France! *(Marches offstage.)*

GINGER. *(Yells to* **EVE.***)* You're nuts, but I don't pay you much. *(After an awkward pause.)* Hello, Tina.

TINA. Hello, Mother.

GINGER. *(Quickly.)* I'm talented too, you know!

TINA. *(Quoting.)* "Talent. Hateful or Grateful?"

GINGER. Huh?

TINA. Just something I needlepointed and hung in my cell.

GINGER. Sorry I didn't visit you. More often, I mean.

TINA. Once would've been nice.

GINGER. I've been so busy redecorating the apartment, winning a Tony, rehearsing my new show, did I mention my Tony? But enough about me. Tell Mommy all about acting prison.

[MUSIC NO. 16C "UNDERSCORE"]

TINA. One thing I did notice, the most ambitious girls were the unhappiest. They were mean, angry, even dangerous. Who brings a switchblade to callbacks?

GINGER. Everyone?

TINA. At first I was scared, so I kept to myself. After a while, I liked my own company. It was nice not needing to be the center of attention or having to show off. I still love singing, but now I sing because it makes me happy. I don't need an audience to do that. *(Beat.)* But look at you, you big Broadway star, you!

GINGER. They say I can play anything, you know?

TINA. That's what I hear.

GINGER. Well, that's what they say.

TINA. I'm surprised to see you're smoking.

GINGER. I don't smoke, silly. But I'm learning. I take a smoking class on Mondays.

[MUSIC NO. 16B]

TINA. Are you happy, Mother?

GINGER. They say I can play anything, you know?

TINA. You didn't answer my question.

GINGER. Did I mention my smoking class?

TINA. Are you, Mother? Truly happy?

GINGER. You tell me. *(Slaps on a big grin.)*

[MUSIC NO. 17 "THERE'S MORE TO LIFE"]

TINA.
ONCE UPON A TIME
ALL I WANTED WAS TO SHINE
BRIGHTER THAN THE STARS
UP IN THE SKY
NOT SO LONG AGO
I WAS PUTTING ON A SHOW
THE ONLY STARS WERE ME, MYSELF, AND I
BUT NOW I HAVE
A DIFFERENT POINT OF VIEW

> I'D LOVE TO SHARE
> ALL THAT I HAVE LEARNED WITH YOU
> THE APPLAUSE IS WONDERFUL, I KNOW
> BUT YOU CAN'T TAKE THE AUDIENCE
> HOME WITH YOU AFTER THE SHOW

GINGER. Well, not all of them, anyway.

TINA.
> THERE'S MORE TO LIFE
> THAN EXCESSIVE SUCCESS
> BEING HOUNDED BY PRESS
> IN A FANCY NEW DRESS
> WHEN YOU APPEAR
> AT A FILM PREMIERE
> AND DO BLOW
> IT'S HEALTHIER ROLLING IN GRASS
> THAN ROLLING IN DOUGH
>
> STARDOM IS BUT A FLEETING REWARD
> TODAY YOU'RE ADORED
> TOMORROW IGNORED
> BUT YOU CAN RELY ON THE MOON
> AND THE MOO OF A COW
> MILKING ITS TEAT IS MUCH SWEETER
> THAN MILKING A BOW
>
> TO THINK ALL THAT MATTERED
> WAS BEING A STAR ON THE RISE
> WHEN I OPENED MY HEART AND MY EYES
> WHAT A LOVELY SURPRISE
> TO REALIZE I'M SOMEONE WHO CARES
> ABOUT SAVING THE WOMBATS AND WHALES
> AND THE KODIAK BEARS

GINGER. Tina, I have no idea what the hell you're talking about, but there is something missing in my life.

TINA. I know, Mother.

GINGER. Do you? Really?

TINA.
> THOUGH YOU'VE LOST YOUR WAY
> PLEASE UNDERSTAND
> YOU'RE NOT ALONE, MOTHER
> GIVE ME YOUR HAND

> *(**GINGER** takes hold of **TINA**'s hand.)*

> I'M HERE

> *(**GINGER** holds both her hands.)*

> I'VE COME HOME
> MOTHER DEAR...
> IT'S YOUR CHANCE TO BE –

GINGER. *(Abruptly lets go of her hands.)* Knock it off, Tina. What are you doing here?

TINA. What do you think I'm doing here?

GINGER. How should I know? I'm a Broadway star, not some Broadway mind-reader.

TINA. Too bad. Then you'd know what I was doing here. Want a hint? It starts with...get outta my way, I'm going to my room.

GINGER. You can't!

TINA. Why not?

GINGER. I sold all your furniture.

TINA. I can make some. I had a whole year of woodshop. We had to build our own sets.

GINGER. *(Turns away.)* Tina, I owe you an apology. The truth is everything is my fault. You're my fault. The way you are, the things you've done. You're not to blame, not for any of it. *(Turns back.)* I'm sorry, darling. If I knew then who I was, I wouldn't have had a child.

TINA. Wow! That makes me feel good.

GINGER. Sit down. *(Gets book.)* There's something you need to know. *(Holds up book.)* Hooked on Fame! The Dark Truth About Ruth...DelMarco.

TINA. You're reading a book? We can't watch the movie?

[MUSIC NO. 17A "UNDERSCORE"]

GINGER. *(Reading.)* "When, as a young girl, Ruth first heard applause, she liked it. She loved it. She wanted more. Very quickly wanting became needing. Soon Ruth was desperate to drink and keep on drinking in round after round of applause. When her show closed after two performances, rather than face living without her nightly dose of the good stuff, Ruth chose to end it all." *(Closes book.)* Ruth DelMarco was my mother. I don't want you to end up like that.

TINA. What about you?

GINGER. It's too late for me, but not for you. You're young and strong. You can fight it!

TINA. Nice try, Ginger, Judy, whatever your name is.

GINGER. Don't you understand? I want you to be happy!

TINA. How 'bout what I want?

GINGER. What you want?

TINA. What you took from me!

GINGER. What? The five bucks I found in your underwear drawer after they hauled your ass off to acting prison?

TINA. My success.

GINGER. What success?

TINA. You turned me in when I was about to have a career.

GINGER. Let's not get nuts, Tina. It was a school show. Besides, I said I was sorry.

TINA. You did not.

GINGER. What do you want from me, huh? Do you want
to live here? Is that it? You want me to feed you too?
Buy you clothes, make you birthday parties, get you
a puppy dog, take you to the dentist? I'm not your
mother! *(Beat.)* Oh.

TINA. And according to my lawyer, you better start acting
like it!

[MUSIC NO. 18 "PARENTS AND CHILDREN"]

GINGER.
YOU'RE NOT MY ONLY REASON
TO EXIST, DEAR
WHEN I THINK OF ALL THE LIFE
I MIGHT HAVE MISSED, DEAR
YES, I HAD A LIFE
BEFORE YOUR BIRTH, DEAR
YOU'RE NOT MY ONLY REASON
TO BE LIVING HERE ON EARTH, DEAR
BEING A MOTHER
IS ONLY A FRACTION
EVEN A MOTHER'S
ENTITLED TO ACTION
DON'T GET ME WRONG, KID
I KNOW THE SCORE
AND I'VE DONE DOUBLE-DUTY
NOW I WANT MORE!
I FED YOU
I DRESSED YOU
YOU SNEEZED
AND I GOD BLESSED YOU
NOW I HAVE A LIFE
I'M MORE THAN A MOTHER!
MORE THAN A WIFE!

TINA.
I AM YOUR KID
AND THERE'S NO GOING BACK, MOM

I'M HERE AND NOW
I THINK I'LL GO UNPACK, MOM
WHATEVER I AM, MOM
I OWE IT TO YOU
SO YOU CAN'T DISREGARD ME
AND DISCARD ME ON CUE
WHO CARES IF YOU AGREE
YOU'RE SHIT OUTTA LUCK, MOM
YOU'RE STUCK, MOM, WITH ME

GINGER.

LET'S BE CALM
LET'S NOT SHOUT
LET'S TRY AND FIGURE OUT
WHAT THIS IS REALLY ALL ABOUT

GINGER & TINA.

WHO'D HAVE THOUGHT
WE'D COME TO THIS POSITION?
MOTHER, DAUGHTER
LOCKED IN COMPETITION

TINA.

AND ALL I WANT IS...

GINGER.

ALL I'M SAYING...

GINGER & TINA.

ALL I HOPE FOR
ALL I'M PRAYING...
IS FOR YOU TO LOOK AT...

GINGER.	**TINA.**
ME	LOOK AT...
LOOK AT...	ME
ME	LOOK AT...
LOOK AT...	ME
ME	LOOK AT...

TINA.

ME!

GINGER.

ME!

TINA.

ME!

GINGER.

ME!

GINGER & TINA.

LOOK AT ME!

PARENTS AND CHILDREN

SO OFTEN LIKE STRANGERS

COMPETE FOR ATTENTION

VIE FOR RESPECT

PARENTS AND CHILDREN

ACTING LIKE STRANGERS

IF YOU TAKE A MOMENT

TO REFLECT, YOU'LL SEE

WE'RE NO DIFFERENT

FROM ANY FAMILY

TINA.

YOU'RE MY MOTHER

GINGER.

YOU'RE MY DAUGHTER

TOGETHER.

LOOK AT ME!

*(***SYLVIA*** enters, unnoticed.)*

TINA. This is how you treat your only child?

GINGER. I learned from the best. My mother didn't care if she had a boy or a girl. She just wanted an audience.

SYLVIA. Poor Ruth. She missed out on so much. *(Smiles at* **TINA.***)* Hello, Tina! Good behavior?

TINA & GINGER. And great reviews.

GINGER. Mama had no choice. Without an audience she was nothing.

TINA. And you? Any motherly instincts still rattling around in there?

SYLVIA. Ginger, if Ruth could only see you now, how proud she would be. She'd love you very much.

GINGER. It's too late. My mother is dead.

SYLVIA. Am I?

[MUSIC NO. 18A "UNDERSCORE"]

GINGER. I don't understand, Sylvia.

SYLVIA. No, my child. Not Sylvia. The name's DelMarco! *(Whips off turban, reveals white hair.)* Ruth DelMarco!

GINGER. Mama? M-M-M-Mama?

SYLVIA. Yes, Ginger. Mama.

[MUSIC NO. 18B "UNDERSCORE"]

After Lita's poisonous review closed my show, I couldn't face anyone, not even my own child. I swam far, far out to sea. As luck would have it, I was rescued by a passing cruise ship. No one recognized me with wet hair. One night I changed my name and sang a couple of songs in the Lido Lounge. They loved me!

TINA. They'll love anything on a cruise ship.

SYLVIA. Soon Sylvia St. Croix was headlining, and calling bingo, in the grand ballroom. One day a producer came aboard and offered me a part in an all-white company of the all-black version of *Hello, Dolly*. I jumped at it. One summer, playing your small town, I spotted you. I was so ashamed of how I pushed you aside, never encouraged you to develop the talent you were born with. *(Beat.)* I just didn't want to share the spotlight.

GINGER. Oh, Mother –

SYLVIA. I still don't.

GINGER. Sorry.

SYLVIA. When I saw my granddaughter, I knew God was giving me a second chance. A chance to come home. Can you ever forgive this silly, selfish old woman?

GINGER. Darling, you're not silly. But why does Tina have to be a star too?

SYLVIA. I see you pushing her aside. I can't let you make the same mistake with your daughter. You'll never forgive yourself.

GINGER. *(Quietly.)* I forgive you, Mama.

SYLVIA. Gingie?

GINGER. Hold me, Mommy!

SYLVIA. Baby!

[MUSIC NO. 18C "UNDERSCORE"]

*(**GINGER** and **SYLVIA** embrace.)*

TINA. Granny!

SYLVIA. Call me Ruth!

GINGER. Why wait so long to spill the beans?

SYLVIA. I didn't want you to think I was hanging around looking for a part in your show because I was your mother or anything.

GINGER. You are going to be in my new show!

SYLVIA. That's awfully sweet of you, dear, but I'm through with performing. What I really want to do is direct!

GINGER. Then you'll direct it!

TINA. What about me?

SYLVIA. She's perfect for the part of your daughter.

GINGER. Sorry. The part's been cast.

SYLVIA. Boo.

GINGER. Talented kid, too. Rachel somebody.

TINA. Well?

GINGER. Well what?

TINA. Does she need an understudy?

[MUSIC NO. 18D "UNDERSCORE"]

GINGER & SYLVIA. Here we go again! *(They bust out laughing.)*

TINA. I want that part!

GINGER. You're not ready for it. Sure, you got rid of the competition once, but have you any idea how many lives you have to destroy to make it in this business?

TINA. I can learn. Teach me?

[MUSIC NO. 19 "RUTHLESS"]

GINGER.
>I REMEMBER THE NIGHT
>I WON MY FIRST TONY
>I THANKED MY PRODUCERS
>SONOCO AND SONY
>I THANKED MY DIRECTOR
>MY HAIRDRESSER, PAUL
>I THANKED ALL THE PEOPLE
>BOTH LITTLE AND SMALL
>AND I ASSURE YOU
>THE TEARS THAT I DABBED
>WERE NOT FOR THE BACKS
>THAT I STABBED
>BE RUTHLESS

TAKE A GANDER AT ME...RUTHLESS
UNCONDITIONALLY...RUTHLESS
THAT'S THE GAME YOU MUST PLAY
TO HIT THE HEIGHTS

SYLVIA.

I GUARANTEE RUTHLESS
PUTS YOU ON THE MARQUEE...
RUTHLESS!
THEY'RE NOTORIOUSLY RUTHLESS

SYLVIA & GINGER.

THOSE WHO HAVE A CAREER, DEARIE

TINA.

BEING SWEET AND AFFECTIONATE
ONLY LEADS TO REJECTION, IT
NEVER WINS YOU A TONY AWARD

GINGER.

LORD YOU'VE HELPED ME
SCRATCH MY ITCH
TO BE FAMOUS AND FILTHY RICH

SYLVIA.

WELL LOOK AT YOU
MY LITTLE BROADWAY BITCH!

GINGER.

I'M FLYING HIGH AND ADORED!

TINA, SYLVIA & GINGER.

WE...RUTHLESS

TINA.

GRANNY, MOMMY AND ME...RUTHLESS

TINA, SYLVIA & GINGER.

TAKE A TIP FROM THE THREE RUTHLESS
LADIES SINGING THIS SONG
CAN THE COMPASSION
THE FASHION IS RUTHLESS

GINGER.
WHETHER YOU'RE YOUNG

TINA.
OR GRAY-HAIRED AND TOOTHLESS

TINA, SYLVIA & GINGER.
THE KEY TO SUCCESS IS...

> *(**LITA, MISS THORN**, and **EVE**, wearing Ginger's
> stained cocktail dress, dance on.)*

ALL.
TO BE TALENTED, YES!
TALENT IS SWELL
BUT YOU GOTTA BE FIERCE
AND FEROCIOUS AS HELL
SHARP AS A TACK
TOUGH AS A COP
EAGER TO CLAW YOUR WAY
STRAIGHT TO THE TOP
YA CAN'T STAND THE HEAT?
GET OFFA THE BUS!
YOU WANT TO BE FAMOUS?
LISTEN TO US 'CAUSE...

WE...RUTHLESS
LOOK AROUND AND YOU'LL SEE...RUTHLESS
DON'T YOU KNOW THAT TO BE RUTHLESS
IN ITSELF IS AN ART?
SO IF YOU'RE SMART YOU'LL
CAN THE COMPASSION
THE FASHION IS RUTHLESS
WHETHER YOU'RE YOUNG
OR GRAY-HAIRED AND TOOTHLESS
THE KEY TO SUCCESS IS
RUTHLESSNESS

GINGER.
>A LOW-CUT DRESS MIGHT IMPRESS
>BUT TO GET THE GIG
>YOU GOTTA HAVE BIG
>RUTHLESSNESS!

ALL.
>THE KEY TO SUCCESS IS...
>RUTHLESS NEH-EH-EH-EH-EH-EH-EH-EH-EH-ESS!

[MUSIC NO. 19A "RUTHLESS (PLAY-OFF)"]

(*LITA and* MISS THORN *dance off stage,* GINGER, SYLVIA, TINA, *and* EVE *dance into place.*)

TINA. I got a great idea. Let's all pile in your limo and plow through Times Square.

SYLVIA. Ooh sounds like fun!

GINGER. I have a show to do, silly.

EVE. I forgot to mention you have a new understudy, so you run along and have a good time.

GINGER. Take off my dress!

EVE. I thought you gave it to me.

GINGER. To take to the cleaners, Einstein. Not to wear.

EVE. By the way, I'm taking the afternoon off.

GINGER. You're not serious.

EVE. I have rehearsal.

GINGER. You're joking.

EVE. I'm your new understudy!

GINGER. You're fired!

EVE. You can't fire me because I quit!

[MUSIC NO. 19B "UNDERSCORE"]

I hate you! I've always hated you! You and your phony ways, speaking lousy French and reading book reviews like they "was" books!

GINGER. Pack your bags and get out!

EVE. Can I keep the dress?

GINGER. Over my dead body.

EVE. Suit yourself.

[MUSIC NO. 19C "UNDERSCORE"]

*(**EVE** whips out a pistol, points it at **GINGER**.)*

GINGER. Eve!

EVE. No. The name's not Eve. It's Lerman! *(Speaks with a distinctively different voice.)* Betty Lerman!

GINGER, SYLVIA & TINA. Who?

EVE. Louise's mother! *(They're still confused.)* Act One!

[MUSIC NO. 19D "UNDERSCORE"]

(Realizing who she is, they gasp.)

EVE / BETTY. I've waited a long time for this. Look at you standing there thinking you're better than everyone else just 'cause you got talent.

GINGER. We are better than everyone else. Honest.

TINA. Stop it, Mother.

GINGER. Tina!

TINA. Do you hear yourself? It's only talent.

[MUSIC NO. 20 "UNDERSCORE"]

GINGER. Pardon e moi?

TINA. *(Comes downstage, addresses audience.)* Talent isn't a bad thing. It's when fame and fortune become more important than what you did for love. When I was using my talent to show off, I did a terrible thing. I can't bring Louise back, but I've learned something. Talent isn't something to cling onto selfishly. Talent is a gift. And like a gift it's meant to be given away with love. Thanks for listening. And God Bless you all.

EVE / BETTY. That's one smart kid you got there.

TINA. Thanks, Betty. *(Distracting her.)* Can I call you Betty?

EVE / BETTY. *(Facing TINA, her back to GINGER.)* Sure, kid.

TINA. *(To GINGER)* Now!

[MUSIC NO. 20A "UNDERSCORE"]

(GINGER grabs for the pistol. They struggle and end up facing upstage. Gunshot. With GINGER holding the pistol, they turn to face downstage and simultaneously check themselves for a bullet hole.)

EVE / BETTY. It's me.

[MUSIC NO. 20B "UNDERSCORE"]

(EVE / BETTY groans and staggers toward the sofa.)

GINGER. Oh, god! Don't get blood on my sofa.

EVE / BETTY. Yes, Miss DelMarco. *(Staggers away from the sofa.)*

GINGER. French?

EVE / BETTY. Ouí, Miss DelMarc – Oh! *(Collapses on floor.)*

GINGER. Tina...

(EVE / BETTY starts to move, GINGER shoots her dead again. She's dead.)

...darling you saved my life.

(**GINGER** *opens her arms,* **TINA** *runs to her. While they embrace,* **TINA** *gets hold of the pistol and backs away, pointing it at* **GINGER**.)

TINA. Now can I be in your show?

[MUSIC NO. 20C "UNDERSCORE"]

SYLVIA. No, Tina! Not this way!

TINA. Back off, Granny, I've killed before.

GINGER. You wouldn't hurt Mommy, would you?

TINA. Oh, so it's back to Mommy, is it?

(**LITA** *bursts in, carrying a bouquet of flowers.*)

LITA. Where's my granddaughter?

(**TINA** *is distracted.*)

SYLVIA. *(Lunges for the pistol.)* Give me the gun, Tina!

[MUSIC NO. 20D "UNDERSCORE"]

(**SYLVIA** *and* **TINA** *struggle and end up facing upstage. Gunshot. With* **SYLVIA** *holding the pistol, they turn to face downstage and simultaneously check themselves for a bullet hole.*)

It's me.

[MUSIC NO. 20E "UNDERSCORE"]

(**SYLVIA** *staggers around.*)

LITA. Why, Ruth DelMarco! You're *not* dead!

SYLVIA. Give me a minute, Encore. Remember, Tina...

[MUSIC NO. 20F "TALENT (REPRISE 3)"]

YOU CAN GO FIRST CLASS
IF YOU'VE GOT TALENT
THE WORLD WILL KISS YOUR ASS
IF YOU'VE GOT TALENT
YOU'LL HAVE IT ALL
WAIT AND SEE
AND ALL OF YOUR TALENT
CAME FROM – *(Collapses.)*

LITA. Ah, she never could sing.

> (**SYLVIA** *pops up, plugs* **LITA**, *they both die.*)

[MUSIC NO. 20G "UNDERSCORE"]

GINGER. *(Wanders in a daze.)* What's happened?

[MUSIC NO. 20H]

Where am? Who am I?

TINA. You're Ginger DelMarco.

GINGER. No. My name is Judy. Judy Denmark. Judy Denmark that's my name! Judy! Judy Denmark!

TINA. Judy?

GINGER. Please, call me Mommy.

TINA. Mommy?

JUDY. *(As if seeing her for the first time.)* Tina?

TINA. Mommy! *(They embrace.)* I knew you'd come back, Mommy. I've missed you so much.

> (**JUDY** *slowly looks around at the dead bodies, then...)*

JUDY. I think we've learned a lesson here, Tina. Now together we can break the chain and once and for all give up show business. Together we'll live a normal, ordinary life. Get your suitcase, sweetheart. It's time to go home!

> (**TINA** *runs toward her suitcase, which is close to where* **SYLVIA** *dropped.*)

As God is my witness, neither I nor my child, shall ever set foot on a stage again. Who needs Broadway?

TINA. You're right, Mother. (*Having gotten the pistol from* **SYLVIA**, *she aims it at* **JUDY**.) There's no money on Broadway. (*Plugs* **JUDY**.) I'm heading for the coast.

> (**MISS THORN** *runs in.*)

MISS THORN. I did it! I quit teaching and I'm back in New York to follow my dream!

> (**TINA** *plugs her.*)

[MUSIC NO. 21 "TALENT (REPRISE 4)"]

TINA.
> I CAN CALL THE SHOTS
> 'CAUSE I GOT TALENT
> THE WORLD IS GONNA PLOTZ
> FROM ALL THIS TALENT
> AND IF YOU DON'T AGREE WITH THIS
> FRANKLY I SUGGEST YOU KISS
> MY ADOLESCENT
> PREPUBESCENT BUM

FREDERICK. (*Offstage.*) Honey, I'm home.

> (**TINA** *runs and opens the door, looks down the hallway.*)

TINA. Frederick?

FREDERICK. (*Offstage.*) Please, call me Daddy.

> (**TINA** *shoots, his body drops, she comes downstage center.*)

TINA.
> HEY, HOLLYWOOD
> HERE I COME!

> *(Slowly…lights fade.)*

The End

[MUSIC NO. 21A "CURTAIN CALL"]

COMPANY. *(Pointing to the audience.)*
> HE RUTHLESS
> UNDENIABLY
> SHE RUTHLESS
> EVERYBODY'S A WEE RUTHLESS
> SOMEWHERE DEEP IN THEIR HEART
> SO IF YOU'RE SMART
> CAN THE COMPASSION
> THE FASHION IS RUTHLESS
> WHETHER YOU'RE YOUNG
> OR YOU'RE GRAY-HAIRED AND TOOTHLESS
> THE KEY TO SUCCESS IS…
> RUTHLESS-NEH-EH-EH-EH-EH-EH-EH-EH-ESS

[MUSIC NO. 21B "EXIT MUSIC"]

> *(After the final bow, as the houselights come up…)*

["I'LL BE AN UNKIE'S MUNCLE"]*

---

* It is unnecessary to credit the singer, but if doing so the credit must read: "I'll Be an Unkie's Muncle"…Ruth DelMarco.